THIS IS OUR BROWN COUNTY

THEN

1800-1900

I0561769

Revering our Past

Helen C. Ayers and Rhonda A. Dunn

Illustrator: John Day

Hardback ISBN: 979-8-9867124-8-2   Paperback ISBN: 979-8-9867124-7-5

This Book Belongs to:

_____

THANK YOU

There have been several people who have helped me produce this book and I would like to acknowledge them.

First of all, I would like to say thanks to my co-author Rhonda A. Dunn, who has worked tirelessly with me in researching the information available at the Brown County History Center. She wrote the final part three of this book to show the types of historical items and events available at the History Center, up the hill from the historic courthouse. She is a very active archivist for that organization which is probably the most active organization in Brown County. She did a spectacular job for this book even though she has been ill.

Others who have helped me were Gary Sisson who is the grandson of Brown County artist Rev. Dwight Steininger. Also, Larry and Lura Baker for taking so many photos for me; my son, Douglas Ayers, employees of the Brown County Democrat for their file photos; my granddaughter, Mercedes Ayers for her teaching me how to put the book together.

To all these helpers I take my hat off to you

FOREWORD

I never liked studying history while I was in high school down in Jackson County. It was such a boring subject, lots of dates to try to memorize and not very interesting to me at all. Since that time and having already written two historical books about Brown County, I find I am rather enjoying writing about history, but I want to recreate history my way, by making it both exciting and interesting.

While I worked as General Manager of the Brown County newspaper for 21 years, I really enjoyed going out into the county to people's homes and interviewing them, getting their life stories, and taking their pictures. I especially enjoyed writing my "Send Offs" that I was permitted to write and put on the op/ed page when someone I knew well had died.

One older gentleman begged me for years to write his send off so he could see what I had to say about him before he died. I told him he had to die first because the dying prompted me to write the stories about my favorite people. Now I am writing about all of Brown County. Perhaps not every single thing about it but I hope I have filled it with warmth and thankfulness to all.

To write this book I researched the memories of a lot of older people, Wikipedia, and my own memories. I realized right out the chute that I could not write only about Brown County. I had to also write several pages about the Indiana Territory, which was a part of the Northwest Territory before it became a state.

Since there is no record now of exactly which family traveled from Corydon to Indianapolis to place our state capital and its records there, I never included anyone's family name in this book. I like to pretend to myself that I'm sitting around a campfire with friends each evening after a light supper, chatting about the day's events, very casually listening to all they say. I like to kick back on a fallen log or big rock or even a quilt spread on the ground, and chat with anyone who wanted to be included. I did that with this book. By placing myself with the wagon train heading north up what is now State Road 135, I could do just that and loved it.

To keep the narrative style of writing going strong, I placed several problems in their path and then helped provide the solution to what the family members need to do, based on what I had learned from my own mother who was a true Appalachian woman who knew how to do many things, and taught those things to me as I was growing up. In doing that I also gave solutions to those problems or expanded on what they had already been told. Since many of those heading north came from the same part of the country from which I had come, and had probably been taught the same as I had been, gives this book's readers a sort of "recipe" for the problems I had thrown at them and which are still relevant today.

This is not a cut-and-dried book, it is a fun book, and a different way of telling stories. Being known as a storyteller, not just an author, I hope you enjoy the book and learn many ways carried down and taught through the ages.

EARLY BROWN COUNTY HISTORY

It would be impossible to write an accurate history of our own beloved Brown County without also knowing a little of the Indiana history prior to trying to write about Brown County, so that is what I am doing now. I have been researching Wikipedia on-line to learn as much about the state's history as is still known after two hundred plus years.

Some of the information was easy to find and interpret but other parts I was interested in was not available, and may never be available, unless someone finds some information to the contrary. I was mostly interested in the route the settlers took to move the capital of the Indiana Territory in Corydon, to the STATE capital of Indiana in Indianapolis.

I have heard so many times in my lifetime living in this county since I moved to Brown County in 1960 when I married my husband, Mickey Ayers of Story (now deceased), that the party traveled the most direct route which, to me, was through Brown County on what is now known as State Road 135. Of course, this route would not be named for more than a hundred years after the move from Corydon, and that also included the fact there were no bridges

4

or roads present on this route at that time. The people moving north may have seen tracks and ruts where the first band of settlers took the state records to Indianapolis and returned the same way, but it would have been more like when the early settlers moved west in their covered wagons.

Since I cannot prove or disprove what I have heard almost all my life I am going to accept that what is now State Road 135 was the most direct route chosen, and the map Rhonda sent me bears this out. When looking at an Indiana map today, any other route chosen would have put the travelers on a route that would have meant they would have had to cross several main rivers and deep streams. By choosing the State Road 135 route they would have had to deal with just three rivers, two of which are smaller than the third. So, State Road 135 is the route I am assuming they traveled, and it was through our county as a lot of the old timers have told me over the years.

Originally some of our residents who came from the Eastern mountains settled in Columbus, or as it was known at the time, Tiptona. The name was changed to Columbus on March 20, 1821. But with all the rivers surrounding Tiptona, the residents there believed a miasma was created that many believed was making the people sick, and some of those people came on across the river and stayed in Brown County.

I tried to find out if there was a ferry across the White River but could not find anything to account for how they left Columbus and came to Brown County, perhaps they waded or rode their horses across the river.

Forgive me if I made the wrong decision on the route they took, but in looking back over 200+ years, I doubt there is anyone who can dispute me, so here we go from this hypothesis.

FURTHER

It is true that Vincennes was the first seat of government in Indiana but that was while it was still known as being a part of the Northwest Territory. It is difficult on my part to think of Indiana being a part of the Northwest Territory since now it is the furthest away East from the Mississippi River and would seem it should have been a part of the Northeast Territory if there was such a thing. But that again is confusing today because we are no longer a part of the Northwest Territory, but if you think about it, that would be correct because the areas to the west of us were still unsettled.

Original Corydon State House

The upper half of the state of Indiana (the Land of the Indians where we got the name) was home to about 12,000 Native Americans of several different tribes while the south half was home to only a few more than 2,632 white people.

On December 11, 1816, Indiana was admitted to the union as the 19th state and In June 1816, 43 delegates met at Corydon to draft the first constitution. Corydon, while not a county seat, was referred to by those living in Vincennes as a Territorial Outpost. Indiana was a territory from July 4, 1800 until December 11, 1813. But after Indiana became a state in 1816, Corydon was truly the first capital of the State of Indiana. The constitution for the newest state was drafted and signed there under a huge elm tree in Corydon which became known as the "Constitution Elm." On August 5, 1816, Jonathan Jennings was chosen as the first governor of the STATE of Indiana by the delegates in Corydon.

It did not take long for the delegates from all over the state to realize that Corydon, too, was much too far away to have our state capital in one of the most southern parts of Indiana in Corydon so a decision was made once again to move our capital, this time to Indianapolis which was more centrally located in the very center of the state and it would make it more accessible for each of the delegates to gather more easily in the state and that is where it is located still today.

Several of the residents of Corydon had floated down the Ohio River on rafts; some from Eastern Kentucky and others from Ohio. They left their boat at Mock's Ferry just south of Corydon and made their way north to the small city of Corydon and stayed there.

At the time the capital was moved from Corydon to Indianapolis, Indianapolis itself was only just beginning to be civil. A few small, sort of decrepit, log cabins had been built alongside the White River which ran right through the city. A few streets eastward of the cabins were designated and named later on and judges and other dignitaries were named to fill those governing posts.

Sale of the lots where the log cabins were located started almost immediately and were grabbed up by those men eager to have a place to bring their families. Some of those streets would stretch farther east later on but when the capital was moved there, it was far different than what many of us can picture today. While small and crude, it was the largest city in Indiana and had the largest population and remains so.

The first meeting of the delegates was held in Indianapolis on November 4, 1816. The constitution written in Corydon would be in effect until November 1, 1851 and it is the one we live by and are governed by today.

The first group returns to Corydon

It had been several weeks that the first group heading to Indianapolis had left Corydon and lookouts watched every day for signs of their return.

Finally, a wagon train was seen making a lot of dust and heading south and the women and children in Corydon were looking forward to seeing the husband/father again after about 12 weeks away.

Late one afternoon the first wagons pulled into the tiny city and the riders began returning to their own homes and waiting families. One of those returning was Mr. Whitcomb. He was one of the last ones to leave that train and head home. Behind him stood a very pregnant, very pretty young woman who lingered some few steps behind him.

His wife ran as best she could run being four months pregnant now with their seventh child to his arms, throwing those arms around her husband and telling him how glad she was that he was home safe. Then she saw the lady a few steps behind her husband and asked him who the woman was. "She's someone I met on the way to Indianapolis, he reported. 'Is she pregnant?" His wife asked. "Yes, she is about 4 months along," he said.

This event had been the remotest thing from her mind since he had left to go north with the state records.

"Well, who is she? Where did you meet her? Is her baby yours?" She continued to ask.

Mr. Whitcomb said only that he met her on the way to Indianapolis before they had crossed White River and she had been with the train since that time.

"So she has been with you all these weeks and now she is as far along in pregnancy as I am. You know you are the father of this child I carry. She had to have become pregnant shortly after you met her, so I assume that child is yours, too." The wife concluded.

Mr. Whitcomb admitted they had had an almost instant affair and she became pregnant. "I'm sorry I hurt you," he said. "I will make it up to you, somehow," he replied with his head hung low and the toe of his boot skipping through the dirt on the ground.

His wife told him in no uncertain terms that he would make it up to her by taking her back to the place he found her. I have worked until I can hardly stand up, and so have our children, preparing foodstuffs to take with us while you have been making love to another woman. Go now and return her to her family. It is up to them to take care of her. You have one week to take her home, leave her and get back here and help me with this move.

"I will find a fresh horse and hitch it to our older covered wagon for us to ride to her home," her husband responded.

WAGONS HO-GIDDYUP

The trip north from Corydon to Indianapolis would take a lot of courage and extreme planning to move all the belongings and government documents that were in Corydon to be moved to Indianapolis 130 miles away. It had been a mere three years since the records had been moved from Vincennes to Corydon. Vincennes would now be the outpost and Corydon the capital. The move would involve not only the records of the newly named state and former territory but a second trip north would be needed to take the families and the furnishings of those men who were being relocated.

There were children, wives, and breastfeeding mothers with babies who had to be accommodated. Each and every additional person or family wishing to move north to reunite their families with the father already there, required lots of thought and planning. There were rivers that would need to be forded and many smaller streams that would have to be crossed in one way or another.

The trip would have to be made when dry weather was upon the little band of residents because flooding and heavy rains would swell those rivers they needed to cross, and slow the progress. So, a lot of planning was taking place and a lot of that planning fell upon the shoulders of the women. And remember there were still many Indians in Indiana at this same time they would have to be prepared to meet along the way or to defend themselves against if they should meet Indians along their way.

The simplest route, looking back over more than 200 years, and knowing what we know today, it would seem to me they would have taken what became known much later as State Road 135, all the way from Corydon to Indianapolis and thus right through the middle of Brown County as some of our old timers have told me over the preceding years. Perhaps their tales were correct.

Of course, as I have stated above, there were no bridges or highways such as we have today to make travel from Corydon to Indianapolis as easy as getting into our cars and driving there in a matter of an hour or two. The moving settlers were breaking new ground with every step they took to the north. It would take days and weeks and much of that time might be spent on the side of the roadways waiting for the water levels to drop in the rivers to where the water courses could then be crossed.

Each family leaving Corydon would mean several covered wagons added to this entourage. They would need one for their young children and wives, especially those who would be breastfeeding babies. Another wagon would be needed to hold their food supplies which they would be busily drying, canning, or preserving in some way while still in Corydon to last the family almost two complete years.

Another wagon would be dedicated to the seed savers of seeds to plant the following spring and summer. Some seeds would be small but others, like potatoes, would take up some space. The same wagon could also be used later in the trip for the barrels which might hold the fish caught as they crossed White River and salted down to preserve them.

And then other wagons would be needed for the horses and mules with some food and spare shoes and supplies for harness mending for those animals and whatever furniture they would be needing when they got settled up in Indianapolis.

It had been a big decision on the entourage's part to move all this equipment, supplies and families along with all the records of the government at one time, and they soon realized at least two trips would be necessary. The state's records must go first separately from the families.

Essentially these same stout women and probably some grown children would be growing and preserving about two years worth of food in the last part of the summer that remained before the start of the trip. That in itself would have been a tremendous amount of work. I could find no notations anywhere that said what day they left Corydon, but assumed it would be late summer or early fall before all the preparations were completed.

They had to eat during the remaining summer months while they were still in southern Indiana, then take enough food along to get them through the first winter and into the growing season that second year before the press for food to keep the families alive and healthy would end.

They would have had to plant two years supply of vegetables that current summer and pick from the woods as much fruit and berries as they could find. All would take a lot of preserving work to keep it fresh and wholesome, but the wife left behind for awhile would most likely have had a few teenage children to help her in this preservation of food.

Drying this food would have made things a lot easier to transport the 130 miles north as whatever they dried would have weighed almost nothing and would last several months if kept dry. They may also have found some seedlings of fruit trees to pack along to plant in Indianapolis when they arrived there to assure the women of fruit in the future for their families.

But the first thing to move were the state's records. Several wagons, maybe four or five would contain the records themselves, along with the personnel going along on this first trip. Another trip taking the families and their supplies would be taken North on a second trip. For the menfolk of the families it would mean a real busy summer of riding horseback or in the wagons.

That second trip, with all its dangers, is the trip I am using for this part of the book.

POSSIBLE SCENARIOS

What I have said here may not be provable, but it is very possible that this is the way the trip went. We are looking back on our history of more than two hundred years so a lot has been lost in the telling and preserving of the stories these early settlers went through, so my tale is probably just as believable as the next person's. I have tried to recreate as accurately as possible, partially based on the trip my own family of parents and eight children made from the mountains of Eastern Kentucky to Indiana in 1948.

A lot of change was seen in our own 350-mile trip, but a lot of it was pretty near the same as this earlier one from Corydon was in a lot of ways. Our trip had to be planned far in advance of its actual happening and we had to prepare for more than just the trip up here. We had a home to come to in Kurtz, Indiana, but for several weeks we had to be prepared to feed a family of ten for as long as it took for us to survive the early winter move. Since we moved north in mid-November we would need almost a year to plant our first garden and preserve our own food. The same amount of time as these settlers we are talking about here today.

And like the women in this story, most of the hard work was given to my Mother who had the eight children including our baby brother who was still breastfeeding to care for. My father was an underground coal miner and was home only long enough to sleep, so the hard work fell to Mother.

For weeks prior to our move north from eastern Kentucky, mother and a hired girl made many kinds of candies and cookies to be used at a going away party for our family. The goodies would have been wrapped and sealed, placed in a miner's round dinner bucket and lowered down into the big dug well just off our back porch to preserve them for later use and to keep them out of children's hands.

Lowering a bucket on a rope down this well was our only means of refrigeration at our home. We also owned a small grocery store down at the end of our driveway. That store had a Coca Cola electric container of icy water for selling soft drinks to our customers. But, as yet, there was no electrification inside our home.

The well was just a bit over 25 feet deep and there was cold spring water pushing up from the bottom. Dad had made a roof over the well and a crossbar from which several ropes holding buckets had been tied. When you wanted something cold to cook for supper, the older boys would check which rope the right bucket was on, pull on the rope and bring it to the top to get whatever it was Mother needed.

I would have to assume that without refrigeration like we have today, the hard- working women in Corydon would have had something like that to preserve foods for their youngsters. The system served us well. But a year or so before we left the mountains, the whole area received rural electric. That is how we were able to keep the water in the Coca Cola Cooler cold. Corydon would not have rural electricity for many years after this story being told. So, I would have to guess they did have a well for water and they had a similar system of keeping milk and other like products cold.

The wife of one delegate, Mr. Whitcomb, was not feeling well after her husband told her he was going north to Indianapolis with the other delegates to take the state's papers there. He would be gone two or three months, he explained, and she would be in charge of seeing that everything they would need for the second trip got done.

Mrs. Whitcomb, (my name for her since there Is no record of any family names in the files), felt worse and worse as the days came for her husband to leave but she said nothing to him about feeling bad.

The morning arrived when he would leave with the others and she kissed him goodbye. It would be a few more days before she was certain, but she was already fairly sure she was pregnant with their seventh child. Morning sickness she had hidden from her husband kept her on her knees almost to noon, but she persevered in her chores.

She had three older sons and three younger daughters to help her, so she put the sons out in the garden area to rake off the dead leaves and twigs and prepare it for planting of sustainable crops she could preserve for the coming winter months.

In the nice rich soil she could walk to the garden and see vegetables sprouting and was elated at her and her son's efforts.

During the wait for vegetables, she scoured all the areas she knew usually had some apple trees and peach trees which would preserve well to take along and to bake goodies for her children as they waited for the dad to reappear.

She did manage to find some fruit tree sprouts and dug them out of the ground to keep and take with her. She also located some places where wild grapes would later grow and put that knowledge in the back of her head to keep.

But each day, she became sicker and sicker, and was worrying about losing this baby she knew she was carrying inside her. Her morning sickness was the worst she had ever had with any of her other children, yet there was a lot of work for her to accomplish before her husband returned. Mrs.

Whitcomb did not have time to be sick. She had to work hard, sick or well.

But time raced on. Vegetables were fresh and vibrant, so she canned all she could gather with the help of her children. The green beans were picked green, then threaded onto heavy twine and hung in their home's attic to dry. They would taste mighty good next winter when everything in the pantry was being used daily and they would be tired of the same old food.

Some five-gallon stone crocks were found to use in pickling some foods, like green beans and corn, and even peaches. Those were easy to do and would last almost indefinitely.

Her children could help her string and break the beans, cut the corn off the cobs once they had been blanched and slice the peaches in halves. Each could then be placed in a crock, salted with coarse salt, add some apple cider vinegar and covered with some boiling water. Insert a clean flat rock down onto an inverted dinner plate, then into the food and let it sink down to the vegetables being pickled so they would remain covered down in the pickling juices. To use, all she would have to do Is rinse the salt off and cook as usual. Pickling would also give her children some vitamins they would need for growth.

Mrs. Whitcomb was also worried about what she could do to obtain milk for her growing younger children who needed it. She had weaned her last baby only a few months ago, but those under six or so needed milk. That was a big worry for her. Finally deciding she would trade her Guernsey cow for three nanny goats solved that worry from her head. She made a deal with a nearby farmer who raised goats to take her trade of the cow for his goats. She believed the goats would provide her and the children with the milk they needed.

The goats would also provide the children with some entertainment along the route. The trip was expected to take a couple of months if all went well. The goats could be on a long tether from the wagon, sleep under one at night, and play with the children to keep them entertained and from becoming bored with their funny antics along the way. If more food was needed for them, one of the sons could show the others how to hold a flat stone in their hand and pull upwards on a grain stalk, removing the grain in the process. With a prairie readily available the goats should not have to have any other special food.

Once the milk problem was solved and the crocks found and filled with the fresh produce to pickle, Mrs. Whitcomb turned to one other item she wanted to take with her and give out as a treat when the time came.

That treat would come from her remaining chickens that ran loose in the yard after laying their eggs in the nests in the chicken house. She saved every egg that was not needed for immediate use and boiled and peeled them. After that she dropped them into a brine she had made to pickle her beet crop.

Most of her beets she had canned because they were very high in nutritional value, others she merely cut off all the tops except she left about one inch of tops on the beets to boil. Once they were boiled and cooled it was a simple matter to slip the skins off. Boiling the results of the now clean beet made an excellent color and vinegary taste to the boiled eggs. Those eggs would be a surprise offering at one of their evening meals when they started north to Indianapolis. Everyone she knew loved pickled boiled eggs, so this was a very special treat for everyone to enjoy. And by their being pickled they did not need to be refrigerated and would last some time.

Despite how bad she had been feeling she had managed to complete a huge amount of work with the help of her children and prepare food for several months to come, maybe even up to almost two years when she got to Indianapolis.

By now it had been some time since he left her to take the young pregnant woman back to her own home, but he still had not returned and she was becoming worried about him.

It would be much later that she learned he had broken an axle on the wagon he took the woman home in, and she had been thrown off the seat onto the ground. She had died before he could remove the wagon from her body and had been buried alongside the road. Her husband had received a bad head injury trying to help the young woman who eventually died in his arms.

He had wandered several days, maybe more than a week around her home base until someone found him wandering along, but incoherent. The people who found him had taken him into their home and had done the best they could for someone who could not answer any questions.

They had found the shallow grave and puzzled out what had happened. He would remain with this family until his real family found him there.

The first teams and wagons were loading up readying to move north before her husband actually returned. The son had had trouble finding his father but then learned he had taken refuge in a home where those living there had attended him. But now he appeared to be in fairly good health. It would be some time after this meeting that the father finally recognized his sons but was ready to accept their help in returning home, so they left the benefactor's home fairly quickly.

The whole wagon train left Corydon soon after the return of Mr. Whitcomb to start the long trek north to Indianapolis

The first test of their preparedness to move north from Corydon would be the crossing of their first river, the Blue River, near today's Milltown. Muscatatuck River would be the second test and much more difficult as this river was much wider and deeper than the Blue River had been. This second river was located just a few miles north on what is now State Road 135 from the town of Salem.

After the Muscatatuck River crossing north of Salem, the really hard test would be the crossing of the White River near what is now known as Brownstown. The crossing of the White River could really slow them down and could even require one to five crossings, depending upon the actual route taken. I have known and made that trip from

Brownstown to my home in southern Brown County intimately having made the trip hundreds of times over the years.

During all of my reading I had heard of the practice of making river crossings possible by laying long timbers cut from nearby wooded areas and placing them longways into the rivers, side by side, but my husband and I had never seen one made like this one until about three years ago. The river's water level in Shieldstown, a tiny burg about five miles northeast of Brownstown, was low and running clear when a couple of boys fishing on a bridge flagged our car down and told us to look down in the water at what they had been seeing. Being young teens, they couldn't name what they saw but it was an old river crossing we were looking at.

Shieldstown was not really a town, but it supplied what several ardent fishermen needed to survive along its shores the same as it does today. On each side of the river the banks had been shoveled down to a slope and in some areas on one of those slopes you could see they had been graveled at some time in the past.

It was possible to take a buggy and horse down one side, stay on the tree poles laid parallel with the flow of the water, then out the other side where that side sloped upward. The crossing poles looked to be about 20-25 feet long. Those poles had been placed in the riverbed many, many years prior to our seeing them, perhaps a hundred or more years prior to the day my husband and I saw the crossing clearly when they became visible after a flood time had passed. It was very interesting seeing this little bit of our history I had read about unfold. (The picture of the tree crossing had to be enhanced to show the detail.)

When the wagon train started crossing the river at this place and time, I'm quite certain a lot of the fathers and young men would have been enlisted to help guide the horses and keep their wheels on the trees felled for this purpose and to help keep the wagons from tipping over as they made their way across the low but still hard rushing river water.

The depth may have been quite low when the travelers crossed it, but with billions of gallons of water pushing against the wagon wheels from the north, it would have been disastrous if even one wagon had toppled over from the pressure exerted by the rushing river water because the wagons would have been top heavy with their loads of equipment and family members and, too, the poles may have become slick with moss.

Regardless of the depth of the water, not many of the women and children would have been strong enough to withstand the push of the rushing water and could have drowned had they left their wagons. And I can imagine the excitement the teenage boys and young men may have felt at this danger. Perhaps, too, some of the older males had taken the smaller children up on their horses and taken them across the river without them having to ride in a wagon that could have toppled in the current.

Right near to this crossing we were witnessing that day on the concrete bridge we were standing upon, there was an old wooden covered bridge spanning the river that has not been used in probably 100 years and beside that wooden one and next to the crossing was the concrete bridge. The covered bridge was being renovated, so we stood on the nice concrete bridge and watched and I imagined a team and wagon crossing right almost under where we stood looking down into the water. I admit I have an active imagination and it was working overtime.

We have not seen that sight again but back when the covered bridge had been completed people could stop using the crossing laid in the riverbed and use the covered wooden bridge. What an advancement that would have to have been to travelers. The covered bridge was the only one for miles up and down the river so everyone had to manage to get to it to cross the swiftly flowing White River which wound around like a snake for long distances. When that covered bridge wore out and needed rebuilding, the concrete bridge was built and then took its place between the covered bridge and the pole crossing. The poles under the water may never be visible again. We will have to wait until the next floodtide and look again. As long as the water level is really low and very clear running, it may be visible.

But if the travelers moving to Indianapolis from Corydon wanted to use State Road 135 all the way, then the Shieldstown crossing would be the best place for them to even consider.

Thinking of their choices, but looking back today, if they had made the trip all the way from Corydon to Brownstown, this would have been the easiest route because if they had taken the jog in the road from Brownstown west toward Bedford and State Road 135 on State Road 50 today, they would have needed to cross this same river at least four more times as White wound around and around before reaching State Road 135, and then as soon as they turned north there, they would have to cross a deep and wide feeder stream.

This route would be state highway 50 today but in the 1940's the road was built up to prevent flooding and I can think of four bridges between Brownstown and State Road 135 in just over five miles of travel as the other bridges were placed over channels of the White River that had occurred over the years.

RECAPPING HISTORY

So, bringing us up to date, Indiana was established as a state in 1816 and Brown County was established a few years later in 1836 with Jacksonburg, now Nashville, decided on as the county seat. Brown County was created by slicing off several square miles from the Jackson, Bartholomew, Morgan and Johnson Counties. Brown County ended up with about 320 square miles in the tradeoff.

During this division of property all the rivers were left in their original locations nearby, and Brown County was given the benefit of having the Salt Creek stay here in 2 or 3 feeder locations to White River in more southern counties. Leaving the three big rivers around Columbus may have been a good situation for Brown County. With the confluence of three rivers and three or more major streams, the town was often flooded. A few years ago now, maybe ten or twelve, water was several feet deep all over Columbus. It was a 500-year flood and closed the city entirely for many days before subsiding. It is still recovering from this incredible flood. Their hospital had at least 14 feet of water in its basement and the entire building had to be evacuated. No entry or outlet from the city was allowed until the water had gone down once again.

Nashville was the second choice for the naming of our county seat as Jacksonburg was the first choice, but it is the one that was kept and the town was renamed Nashville in late 1870. It is believed by many that the name of Nashville was chosen because so many of the new residents were from Nashville, Tennessee. With a population of just about 15,000 in the entire county, only about 700 residents actually live in Nashville even though it is the only incorporated town in the county.

The largest township, area-wise in the county, is now Van Buren Township in the southern part of the county. (I call it God's Country). At one time it was much smaller but when the site for the largest state park in Indiana was chosen, it was to be here in Brown County they chose, with just slightly over 15,800 acres, entirely forested, that was considered.

That state park is the largest and busiest in the state's park system and is located less than one mile east from Nashville. It has three entrances, one in the south part on State Road 135 for horseback riders and campers only. The north entrance on SR 46 East has a dual lane covered bridge entrance which is super nice, historically, and well maintained but limits the weight limit on every vehicle crossing into the park. The third entrance on the west side of Nashville on State Road 46 West is for the normal flow of all other traffic. All the entrances today are made through a log cabin gate which provides job opportunities for several older residents in the seasons.

Many but not all of the acres to establish the Brown County State Park and other state-owned properties were forcibly removed from the prior owners in Van Buren Township. Today there is only a small fringe of privately owned land around the southern and eastern edges of the state park. All the rest of the acreage was removed from the tax rolls.

Also removed from the county's tax rolls was Johnson Township, just to the west of Van Buren Township. When the various governments decided to establish the Hoosier National Forest, another several tens of thousands more of acres were removed.

At almost the same time other acres were removed for establishing the Yellowwood State Forest in 1940, and even in later years, more acres were taken for the Charles Deem Wilderness Area, and finally the Monroe Reservoir required even more land to be removed and people displaced. The Deem acreage did not involve privately owned property.

All these selloffs of land in the southern part of Brown County reduced its acreage considerably but when it had to become home to the eastern half of Johnson Township where Elkinsville and Uno were once located and all in between those areas to Story, Van Buren grew in size of acreage again so now we have become the largest township, not in population but in size, although thousands of acres of the land is under water.

These projects would nearly break the back of the Van Buren residents as those dollars earned by the rightful owners was placed in a bank account with the owner's names on it, and they were told to move out. With no recourse, those homeowners generally moved to the cities where they normally worked and their homes and barns and other outbuildings were bulldozed down and most were burned. Bridges leading West were removed or demolished and left in or nearby the creek.

The town of Elkinsville was located in Johnson Township and would later become known as the "Town That Was," because it no longer was a town. A book has been written by former resident Bob Cross but may be out of print now. The former residents of this little town, which was a viable country town with a grocery store, church and a grade school and several homes, meet each year at the old Elkinsville location for a reunion in October and to get reacquainted with their old friends.

After that exodus happened, Johnson township, now with less than 100 residents, was enjoined on the east side with Van Buren Township. The township was removed from the maps to make room for the Monroe Reservoir which was designed to provide a water supply for the Bloomington area in Monroe County.

The few residents living on the western side of the reservoir that was not covered by water, was tacked on to the southwest side of Washington Township. Not one access point was made for the folks in Van Buren or Brown County when the reservoir was completed and the residents of Van Buren lost their only outlet to the west when the water eventually covered the entire Johnson township except for perhaps a dozen or so homes situated in higher locations.

Today, without that road to the west, in flood times we cannot leave our township that way, nor can we drive south because Salt Creek floods State Road 135 in several locations. We cannot go east toward Bartholomew County because we cannot get past Stone Head and Pike's Peak for the high water there.

That leaves going north on State Road 135 toward Nashville the only possibility. All the residents know that when they see the Van Buren Grade School on the right as they head on up 135 near Stone Head and have seen high water in that little stream alongside the road, they should turn right onto Valley Branch Road. The reason for this turnoff of 135 is because when we arrive at Camp Roberts there are four very low, usually flooded rip-rap places you would have to cross and take your life into your hands to cross after any heavy rain.

I recently learned the state was considering fixing the four locations in Camp Roberts that would allow us to go directly north on SR 135 without having to ford water. I recently went that direction though and the only improvements I could detect were the rip-raps had been repaved, not raised. State Road 135 is considered a "scenic" highway and will probably never be raised to make driving easier.

Turning onto the higher elevated Valley Branch Road by the elementary school prevents a lot of turn-arounds when drivers get to Camp Roberts. Valley Branch is not as low as State Road 135 and doesn't usually have running water across it so we can reach State Road 46 east of Gnaw Bone and get out that way. Essentially when Salt Creek floods, we stay in our homes and just wait for the high water to recede. We cannot go to our jobs or get out of the county in any normal direction. So we cook, watch TV, read or eat pop popcorn to while away the hours until the water recedes. Neither fire departments nor ambulances can reach us by highway. The only way to get out in a health emergency is by air. That is just one way of life that makes us Brown County. We have learned to adapt to our circumstances.

During the building of the Monroe Reservoir the federal government spent several million dollars building a series of bridges and raising the ground level for the one gravel road out of the floodway to the west toward Blue Creek Road. That road went only a couple of miles and served two or three residents then ended in a creek with nowhere else to go.

If it had continued right at that point up what was known as Miller Ridge and continued on to State Road 46 West just below Mike's Dance Barn, it would have been great for those of us who have to go miles out of our way to go to Bloomington which has plenty of our water, but no way for us to easily shop and visit there.

I think that area on top of Miller Ridge would have worked well as an industrial center for Brown County, which in turn, could have prompted some businesses to be built on the side next to the town of Story, like small motels, fast food places or gas stations, etc.

The residents in the lower third of Brown County now had to go several extra miles even in sunny weather to find an access point to the lake to go fishing or visiting friends in the Crooked Creek area or to get to the city of Bloomington. When the tourist season is upon us in Nashville, and traffic is backed up for miles, it is a long, long way for us to get to Bloomington, so we stay home until the water recedes. This has been a sore talking point to the Van Buren people ever since their land was removed from their possession.

At the beginning of the last century, the beauty of what was left to become Brown County was discovered by now world re-known artists. They began coming here to see the lovely leaves as they changed during their seasons and those beautiful images were put onto canvas by their designers and displayed and sold.

One of the better-known early artists was T. C. Steele and his wife, Selma. They built the House of the Singing Winds, just down a country road to the south in the center of Belmont west of Nashville, high on the ridgetop where each could do his/her paintings. The wife also loved yellow Easter lilies and spent years developing the landscape around their home with thousands of these blossoms.

After they returned to their homes in Indianapolis and other areas, dozens of other artists followed them. Many stayed with the Steeles and others stayed in rooming houses which were springing up there in Nashville.

It was a common sight to be driving down a country road during the last mid-century of about 1920 to 1960 and come upon one or more of the artists sitting on their little folding stools along a highway that had little traffic or in the edge of your lawn, with an easel in front of them as the artist viewed and painted what they were seeing. Later, they began coming in droves and many became very famous around the world for their artistry.

From the early 1900s through 1930 or thereabouts, the doings of the artists became the lifeblood of the jobs and earnings to be made in Brown County and was also the start of the many art colonies still alive and thriving today in Nashville.

There are major art galleries, and small ones, in Nashville as well as several dubbed as guilds, but all showing the wares of the older artists as well as the later day ones. One shop specializes in chainsaw art.

Photographer Frank Hohenberger captured many of our activities with his camera. Many of his photographs are on sale or just for viewing in Nashville. Hohenberger's entire collection is owned by Indiana University. His photographs are from only one of two noted photographers living in Brown County at the time I arrived in 1960.

The other photo-artist was named Otto Ping. Though not as well known as Mr. Hohenberger, he lived just out of Pike's Peak to the south on Poplar Grove Road. Otto continued to take photos for many years of the local people whereas Mr.

Hohenberger took pictures of families, homes and other places that showed the destitution or hopelessness that were rampant in this area at his time of visitation here.

These destitute people were the remnants of the very earliest settlers to move here from the Eastern Kentucky areas as my folks did later on. I chronicle them in my first book, "Appalachian Daughter."

Mr. Ping said he stopped taking photographs on glass plates in the early 1940s when Eastman Kodak invented a camera anyone could use, essentially putting him out of the photography business. The Ping families were early settlers who had once lived in Columbus but moved to Brown County because it was safer, healthwise they believed, than Columbus.

Mr. Ping then turned to operating a canning factory there at his home farm. He would ask anyone who wanted certain vegetables canned at his factory to let him know early in the spring so he would know which vegetables he should plant. The late Norma Crouch had copies of several of his photos and an original label from a can he had produced that asked people to let him know what they needed him to produce and preserve that summer.

Many residents of the early Brown County were attracted to this place because it looked a lot like their homes they had left behind in the Carolinas, Virginias, Ohio and Kentucky. These people were poor, but they were proud.

Their being very stout people, they succeeded where many others would fail. Each knew how to raise a garden with the help of the family, how to grow and harvest hogs for their meat and live off the land killing squirrels and rabbits and other game food; catching fish from the nearby creeks to feed their families. They were a sturdy bunch of people and many of their descendants are still here today. I chronicled these late 1800 settlers in my second book, "The Stuff of Legends". Those two books along with this one you are now reading, make up my trilogy of history books about Brown County. I'm not aware of anyone else writing so many history books about this wonderful county but I'm glad I got the chance to do it. Several people had urged me to write more about it. But with these three books, I cover the events from 1800-NOW.

I brought an aunt to visit Brown County one day a few years ago and spent some time with her up in the Brown County State Park. She was amazed at how much the park area looked like the land she and my family had left down in Eastern Kentucky. "I know now why you like it here so well," she said, "It looks like "home" to you also. She was correct, it does look like home to me and remains so today all these years later.

Let's jump ahead a bit and see what is going on in Nashville

Writer Ernie Pyle lived in Nashville for a time during his war correspondent years as have several other television stars. Several of our residents are writers, poets, weavers, etc. making things the public loves to use and read.

A large number of our homes are constructed of logs, reminiscent of the earliest days in Brown County and some as a reminder of the homes the residents had left behind to homestead again here in this beautiful area.

These log homes can be deceiving. They are as modernized as can be done on the inside with all the amenities needed and loved by the richer homeowners we are seeing more of today, who gave up the same things found in their stick-built regular homes in exclusive neighborhoods.

You can find master log home builders here or you can order a pattern and have a local sawmill cut the logs for you and sometimes they will even construct the cabin.

Nashville is becoming a sprawling town made out of 3-story buildings which house not only artworks but also have rooms to rent, places to eat and gifts to be had of all kinds, but many log cabin shops and homes are still found right here in Nashville. Most of the merchants try to keep a good supply of Brown County Made items in their shops, but some have lovely gifts from other places as well for sale that would please many buyers.

During this past Christmas season there were so many objects sitting out on the sidewalks for sale that had not been shown before that it was great to walk or drive through the town and just keep in mind what you wanted to buy. There are many wooden benches set out on the sidewalks of town so you could stop and rest for a spell, maybe eat an ice cream treat, drink a cup of coffee, and just watch the people walking by and maybe speaking to you. It is really, really fun.

Many of the merchants stay open all winter long, but maybe with shortened hours, that it would be nearly impossible not to have a good time in Nashville at any time of the year.

Now that virtual shopping is taking off here on a website called Brown County Souvenir.com it is even easier to get your fillup of Brown County items right from your favorite seat in your own home. But it is a lot of fun also to visit Nashville and/or Brown County State Park and mingle with millions of other visitors to Brown County.

If you don't want to mingle with that many people and you want to visit Nashville and you need to make reservations for accommodations, I would advise you to make them as early in the year as possible. There are several lodging places to rent, including those small cabins inside the Brown County State Park, rented out through the Abe Martin Lodge.

I have seen the time in years past where the traffic was backed up nearly all the way to Interstate 65 in Columbus to the extent the state police would not allow anyone else to leave I-65 to head this way, and about the same distance to the west toward Bloomington. Traffic backups are not quite that heavy now as a lot of parking lots and streetside bathrooms have been built in Nashville.

Also, many motels are here and close to 300 bed and breakfasts are here so that has helped with the traffic problem along with our moving from a one stoplight town to—count em—three now in use.

But when the settlers were moving from Corydon to Indianapolis, they did not have all the options we have today. By the time they reached Nashville from Corydon they had put many miles and several weeks of travel behind them.

The most tired of the moving crew were the women and children, of course. They were exhausted and had just about had all the excitement they could stand. All of them wanted a warm bath and some place to lay their heads for a sleep while someone watched their children, especially the ones with very young babies.

When they arrived in Nashville, they were relieved and delighted to find there was one or maybe two very crude and plain boarding houses in the tiny backwoods town where some of these needs could be met. The mothers almost crashed into their beds that did not rattle and sway when they saw the featherbeds beaten high and flat under warm covers for their bodies. A tub of hot water would have been a real treat or even a dip in nearby Salt Creek which had both deeper and lower pools of water.

These people they met in Nashville were the survivors of the original movers from the southeastern states and now those from the lower part of the Indiana Territory. They all had something in common with the others.

While they had waited for their husbands and perhaps older sons to return to Corydon from the first trip to Indianapolis, there were many chores for the women and younger children to do to be ready to move to the next little back-woodsy town of Indianapolis which was just being formed itself. The first homes were crude log homes that hugged White River which runs right through the town.

Out in the country where the women and children lived near Corydon, they were busy preparing enough food to last the family all the way through the coming winter and most of the next summer. This was a daunting task.

They spent lots of time in their gardens as long as summer lasted, picking green beans to make shucky beans or beans to shell out and dry to make soup beans, corn, tomatoes and potatoes. From the nearby woods the children were delegated to bring their mothers all the grapes, apples, peaches, pears and any other fruit they could find. It now being November, some of the fruits were already out of their season, but she would preserve all this bounty her children could find in glass jars or dry it to take on their journey.

My own mother could make a big meal out of the fruits and berries we brought to her. She would place some of the bounty in a good-sized pot, add sugar and a little water, then add the fruit and/or berries. When all this was cooking, she would drop dumplings into the pot, put a lid on the whole shebang and wait for it to be done. Therefore, I am sure these women preserved everything their children brought to her from the nearby areas so she would have been able to do the same thing as my mother. They were each taught by their mothers to take care of their families before anything else.

These women and their neighbors probably each butchered a big fat hog and made lard and sausage to take with them by making sausage balls, frying them, placing that meat in clean jars and pouring the grease made from the frying over the sausage balls to seal them and then put a sterile lid on each.

Some of the meat, such as whole hams and slabs of bacon, would have been preserved with a salt combination my mother used. I'm not sure of any recipe other than that it contained canning salt, ground hot pepper and some brown sugar, then patted onto the slabs of meat, wrapped in heavy paper and allowed to age.

Usually, the hams would have been hung from the ceiling in our mouse-proof garage area, or at other times simply laid in there flat on a table with the wrappings on them.

The families may have had to go into the wooded areas around Corydon and drive the hogs to be slaughtered to their homes as we did in Kentucky. The Kentucky farmers knew how long it took an old sow to have her piglets so he knew just when to put her to the boar. After the piglets were born and weaned, the gates to their pens were left open and they were left alone to wander into the mountains to eat the mast (berries, roots, acorns) they found there until the fall killing time. At this time and place we don't know if that practice continued in Corydon, but I presume it did. My fraternal grandfather was murdered in Kentucky over hogs of this type in a feud with his neighbor.

When the meat wrapper was opened in order to cook it, all the seasoning had to be washed off or it would have been too salty to eat but would not have lasted long if the recipe for preserving meat had not been used. I know mother tried buying seasonings for our meat from the local grocery store but neither she nor the rest of us liked the commercial blend so we went back to the way we had always done it.

Perhaps these women from Corydon did much the same way as we did to preserve food as we all came from the original eastern coastal states to begin with and were trained the same way mother had been taught, and we children of hers as well, and now I have taught my two sons the same things I was taught.

I recall one year the neighbors at Story wanted to butcher some hogs. There were five families to the best of my memory now. The guys took a couple of pickup trucks to one's farm and brought back two hogs, which we were ready to butcher as soon as they returned. That was so much fun for the younger set to see and participate in that we decided to do some more. The day was still young so why not? The same guys went back to the farm and brought three more hogs to us. On their way back with those hogs a deer committed suicide by jumping in front of a bullet and was brought back also.

So that day these families butchered five hogs and one deer and started the process of making lard outside in a black iron kettle over an open fire while the others remained in the garage, rubbing my mother's recipe (as closely as I could remember it) on the meat and wrapping it for aging.

My husband and I were the only ones there, even though three of the people with us were much older, who knew how to remove a hog's head from the body but we got the job done for the others to see.

I can imagine the Corydon women and the children picking green beans, stringing them on strong twine. Then they did the same thing for any fruit the children brought to her from the woods, then hanging everything in an airy safe place for the fruit and beans to dry, thus making shucky beans and dried fruit that would last for months if kept dry. This bounty would weigh almost nothing compared with their early life as a green bean or plump fruit. This was a job I loved to do when I was a child.

Berries could be preserved in this manner also, usually by placing the berries one layer deep in a shallow cardboard box or pan and leaving them in a sunny place to dry where the birds could not get to them.

Some other things would be pickled and placed in stone crocks, the contents weighted down with a heavy clean stone, with the top covered by a clean cloth of some kind, then secured firmly in place. The vinegar would help keep not only the vegetables edible but would keep their children healthier. To eat the shucky beans, they just had to be soaked overnight then cooked the next day until softened and rehydrated, then adding some of the lard and any kind of fat meat they may have had on hand for seasonings. Cornbread would be baked to go with the beans.

She could have also dried some of her white potatoes and yams and canned others. I personally don't like canned potatoes but if you are hungry or need to feed an army of small fry, they will do. Had she raised carrots, as we do occasionally, they can be kept alive for several months if placed in a box of soft dirt or sand by sticking the carrots root down into the soil and pulled out to use.

If they wanted onions, they could have pulled the ones left in the garden from the summer and hung up in handfuls to dry also. The top bloom of the onion plant may have had a ball of seed onions up there which would have been priceless where they were going. Make sure to give these bulbs to the seed savers of the group.

When ready to use these wonderful additions to their food stuffs, if she had cut off the whole root system of onions and planted those back into fresh dirt in a box or container of some type, they would have raised even more of the same except they would get about five or six green onions in their place. If they planted the root systems of the green onions, they would have produced large onions, thereby keeping that vegetable growing indefinitely.

This idea works just as well in a family garden plot too. Use an onion hoe and pull the dirt away from each plant to grow big onions or hoe dirt to the plant to have green onions. An onion hoe has two wide flat prongs with a slot in between them for hoeing. You may have to consult a hardware store to find one or attend a farm auction and buy one there.

There were so many things she would have been able to do to prepare for her family's move to Indianapolis when that time came and I'm sure she tried every method available to her. If someone had been raising bees for the honey she might have bartered something (like a jar of pickled eggs) she had for a few jars of honey. It may have hardened in the jar as they went along, but it can be reconstituted easily by warming the jar of honey in a pan of hot water. It is very difficult to kill honey. Preparing for a two-year hiatus of food would be a monumental job for anyone but women were raised by their parents to be self-sufficient back then.

Women were very resourceful at that time in our history, just as they were down in the mountains of Eastern Kentucky where I and many others who live here now came from. I have always said that mother could have made life a lot easier for Generals Patton and Eisenhower with her backwoods mountain knowledge and ability to organize.

While the women were preparing food to last two years, their husbands were busy too, seeing to their horses' feet and hooves and making sure if they needed shoeing it could be done before they left home or here in Nashville or somewhere else just as well. Checking all the harnesses would have been a crucial job.   And they would check the wagon wheels and axles also to make sure they were still in good condition and greased well.

One job the older boys would have been taught, especially the ones who had gone north with the first contingent, would have been to see to the horses at days end. They could now make surrounds (ramudas) for the horses to stay in at night, making sure they were near a water source. They would have to remove the harnesses and check the horse bodies for sores caused by the rubbing of the harness. If they found sore places, the next day they would place a heavy blanket between the horse and the harness. Everyone except for the very youngest had a job to do.

They were not quite as back woodsy as they looked and seemed elated that many of their requirements were met here in Nashville when they managed to arrive here. After a day or two's layover, most of this traveling band were rested and ready enough to complete their journey on to Indianapolis. Another three days or so and they should arrive at their destination.

So tenacity and ability to do what was called for is what makes us unique as a county. We came from sturdy stock and we knew the triumphs of being able to survive a 130 mile trip with family, horses, children, and all the worries that were anticipated.

My family traveled about 350 miles to reach our new home down in Jackson County in 1948. That was much longer than the trek to Indianapolis from Corydon and in November that year (the same as they.) Dad made some early trips without my family bringing our work horses, farm implements and other bigger, heavier things before bringing us up here. But Dad had a big flatbed farm truck he bought as a World War II kit, put it together and built side rails on it. That's what we moved in, not a covered wagon.

Dad would have been just as well off to have sold those things to his neighbors in Kentucky because farming 100 acres here was far different than "farming" a little patch of corn and pumpkins on a steep hillside down there. He immediately realized the next spring the difference and sold the horses and bought our first tractor.

While they were in Nashville, the husbands and/or teenage boys did what they could to help as many of their mothers, sisters and other females find places to cleanse themselves of the road dust that had accumulated on their persons and clothing during the march up State Road 135 from Corydon to Nashville. They looked for pools of water in the nearby Salt Creek where they could wade in and take baths and bathe their children before they continued on their journey.

The luckier families had found what little support they could find in the tiny town of Nashville. Not too much was available but the creek, though the water was cold, at least it provided a place to clean their bodies and their clothing, and the women were glad to find any help at all.

The women had made new batches of lye soap to use on their journey. Some of it was used to wash the lice and filth from both their own and the children's hair and bodies. Lye soap was made by heating water in a black kettle over an open fire, adding fat from either frying or cooking pigs, and then the wood ashes.

They may not have realized it, but by adding these wood ashes they were making lye, but they would know all that was necessary and that was that it worked as a cleaning soap. It would be poured into trays or shallow boxes and allowed to "set up," then sliced into usable pieces.

Let's return here again to our narrative.

THE CARAVAN
MAKES IT TO BROWNSTOWN

The caravan had made it across the first two rivers they needed to cross with no problems, and the White River just northeast of Brownstown at Shieldstown in Jackson County, with only minor mishaps.

One of the younger boys told his mother about the huge catfish he had seen in the river at Shieldstown. It was really, really big, he said. At that revelation the mother of that one began emptying a wooden barrel of its contents of dried potatoes and told the boys to go fishing, take some friends, and catch all the catfish or other types of fish they could.

When they returned to her with a huge catch of fish, she bade them to gut, scale, de-head them and get them to her as soon as possible. She had instantly seen the bounty these huge fish made to their dried and pickled store of food. She fixed a huge amount of the fish for their supper that evening and shared with her neighbors. Some of those catfish weighed in at 50 plus pounds each as they still do today.

While Mrs. Whitcomb was frying fish that evening, another family was busy making and cooking hushpuppies. Easy to make and quick to disappear,

Long John Silvers restaurant may have used their recipe in later years. All it takes is a big deep pan of hot lard or oil; cornmeal and a tiny bit of flour, salt, and milk to hold it all together. Roll out a big spoonful in your hands to shape each ball pretty tightly, then drop the hushpuppies in the hot oil for a few minutes until they are nice and brown and enjoy. Other families were making macaroni and cheese and other wonderful and welcomed dishes to add to their supper.

At the conclusion of their culinary feast that evening, Mrs. Whitcomb brought out her big jug of pickled boiled eggs. They were an instant hit and were enjoyed down to the last bite. No one but her children knew she had pickled all those eggs using some of the beets left in her garden, but they sure were glad she had made this treat.

Mrs. Whitcomb had added the remaining cleaned fish to that barrel she had emptied and poured a heavy amount of salt over them to keep them from spoiling. What a boon those fish made for the families in their nutritional requirements.

The boys may have shot the fish with their muskets as nearly every boy child over the age of 12 owned one, or their father had one, or a bow and arrow they had made, or gigged them with sharp sticks, or even snared them. But probably they would have merely seined them in a seine they had brought with them. Three or four young men working together could catch many large fish this way. At any rate, they collected many fish that day. Any of these methods would have been difficult because the water deflects the images and it is hard to hit something.

JUST FOR FUN, LET'S EXPLORE SNARING FISH

The men and boys around the Story community used to snare suckers, a carp-like fish, using a cane pole with a heavy cord on it, and a copper wire noose (or snare) on the lower end. These fish were like salmon, they returned every year upstream to spawn in Salt Creek. The fishers would tie a heavy nut from a bolt or a small rock with a hole in it to help maneuver the snare over the fish's body. Once the snare circled the fish, they would grab the pole and sling the heavy fish out onto the banks of the creek.

Whoever was IT (had gotten hit) had to remove the fish from the snare, place it on a limb stringer that had been prepared to keep it from slipping away after it was placed in the water. This would keep the fish cool until quitting time. It sounds difficult but it was fairly easy to do. (My nine-year-old son caught eight one day, and they were so heavy he could not lift them.)

When the fish was thrown on the creek bank, if you were IT and standing there not watching what was coming at you, you would get slapped on the chest and covered with the ripe eggs that would be expelled from the fish from that blow to you.

Perhaps the early settler boys prepared something similar to this.

The sport only lasted about two or three days, then even a small rain would roil the water and the fish could not be seen again until the next year. The bounty of fish would be cleaned and shared around the Story neighborhood with any widows who liked the fish but could not snare them by themselves. All would set to after arriving home with their catch to clean them. This was done by removing the scales by scraping then fileting the meat. The guts and head would be removed, and the fish turned upside down with the skin still intact. A sharp knife would be used to score (slice) the fish from the heavy meat all the way to the skin about every quarter inch or less, but not through the skin to prevent choking on this bony fish. A large portion of the catch were immediately eaten at a neighborhood fish fry as described in preceding paragraphs, or frozen for later use. None went to waste.

The men and older boys had prevented one of the top-heavy covered wagons from slipping off the logs planted in the river at the crossing at Shieldstown.

It took all the available muscle power to keep that wagon from being pushed sideways by the swift water off the slippery logs which were now covered with a moss-like substance and therefore was slick, similar to cobblestones used extensively in foreign countries. The cobblestones are very rough but very effective when used as paving stones over in Europe and they last for centuries. These battered, weary souls knew nothing of cobblestones, they just knew the going was very rough. But the force of the rushing river water, though low, carried a lot of power so it was touch and go for a while, but masculine muscle prevailed.

The wagonmaster in the moving game had an excellent idea about the next crossings they would have to weather on the northern side of White River. Several men and older teen boys were sent a goodly distance ahead from the White River crossing to the next stream they could find which would be over a very narrow feeder stream into the White River. Since there was no such thing as a chainsaw back then, the males gathered together their axes, crosscut saws and a few hammers to do this job.

Their experiences with narrow crossings were remembered when they came to the White River feeder streams. They had had to lay over for two days to let all the men and horses try to get a wagon out of the narrow stream at one of the smaller rivers they had crossed. They worked endless hours, having to completely unload the wagon on the side of the road to lighten the load, pry the wagon up from the muddy bottom which acted like quicksand, and use a string of horses to pull it out of the mire. Then it had to be cleaned, reloaded and moved to a different place in the river to cross there.

They were told to cut several timbers that could sufficiently span the width of the feeder stream and split a couple of logs, probably with wedges and a sledgehammer, to lay side-ways over the span to provide some more secure ways for the wagons and the horses pulling them, to cross the narrow streams. Most of these feeder streams were too narrow for the wagons to enter the water and then have to be turned slightly to exit on the farther side. So, they built these temporary bridges. It was a tricky job but one that solved the primary problem of crossing these narrow streams.

There were tepees seen across the first open field they came to that were set at the other end of the field nearly into the woods. No Indians were seen but everyone in the wagon train was nervous about just the site of the tepees. It paid off because that very night two horses disappeared from the remuda and were never found again. It was assumed the Indians had led them away with their feet encased in a burlap-like sack, without making any noise to awaken the teenage watchers. But it paid off by making everyone on the wagon train more observant of the danger and they did not lose any more horses.

But building the small portable bridges served to all to see how safe and easy it made the small crossings so much simpler.

Once all the wagons were across the first stream, the wooden bridges were pulled away from that location, placed on a spare wagon or hitched to horses to be pulled along the ground, and taken ahead of the journeyers to the next crossing, sometimes not that far away. It worked very well for the narrowest streams feeding into the White River. The wider streams where the wagons could enter, turn if needed and then exit were less problematic, but having these "bridges" available to span the really narrow streams was a novel and genius idea by the leader. It saved the wagons a lot of time getting over the many smaller streams.

The farther away from the river they traveled, the fewer the feeder streams appeared on the horizon, so they finally abandoned the temporary bridges. If they needed to do so they now knew what was necessary. As long as the streams were wide, they could be waded, or the wagons could be driven across the smaller ones without very much problem.

With our knowledge of the streams in Brown County today, we know that there were not that many streams where the small bridges would be needed. The wagon train would reach almost to Nashville before seeing really small streams so they could be crossed without a bridge. Some places it was prudent for the drivers of the wagons to use the nearby sometimes dry creek beds as their route.

The wagon train was spotted approaching Brown County in the South. In another two or three days they would be in Nashville. They had made very good time once they got past the river bottoms north of Brownstown.

Many times in the early days of Brown County, people with horses and wagons could pay their county taxes by taking gravel from the nearby stream and placing it on the roadway that would eventually, in years to come, be paved. This idea had helped speed the wagons on their way. It opened areas for them to cross after the gravel had been removed and placed on the roadways of the future.

The other thing the wagon train had had to watch for were more of the Indians they had been told they would probably see before this trip was over. It had been a really safe trip in many ways getting from Corydon to Nashville.

The last leg of their journey would see them leaving Nashville and heading north towards Indianapolis, still on State Road 135. The planning took longer than the doing but it paid off.

There would be only a one steep hillock in their way going north from Nashville. The first one would be about a mile in length but certainly not in height. It was a steady pull to go north on the hill just at the northern edge of Nashville towards Bean Blossom Creek. About one mile up this hillside was the highest point the wagons would encounter from there to Indianapolis.

Once the wagons reached the top of this one long hill and started down the other side, they would be at the place where the last remnants of the last Ice Age stopped and left its load of miscellaneous soils, creating this hill as well as many of the hills to the south of Brown County, almost to the Ohio River.

My husband, Mickey Ayers, was a water well driller as a professional and one year he was drilling a well at Fox's Corner which is located to the east on this hillside. He loved checking the stuff he pulled from the bottom of the wells and when our boys or other young children were present watching him drilling, he became a knowledgeable geologist. He explained as he combed his hands through the "cuttings" what he could know to these younger people. Cuttings were the detritus of the formations he was drilling through left there by that last Ice Age.

He was surprised when he combed through the cuttings at Fox's Corner one day to discover a piece of wood from 105 feet down in the well.

For a long time, he kept this piece of wood in a camera film case I gave him. You could see the tree rings clearly, so he knew the tree was at least 105 feet down in the ground, left there when the ice had melted after pushing up this hillside. Mickey often found bits of gold and many other types of stones in his cuttings. It fascinated the children who crowded around to hear him talk or to just be allowed to play in the mud he extracted from the wells. Those children loved MUD.

He opened the film case a long time after that to show someone who was visiting us and poured the tiny piece of wood out into his hands. It had dried out completely by then and when it met the air in our house and was touched, it disintegrated completely to dust.

But none of this history about the Ice Age was known by the travelers of yesteryear nor to some of those residents living here today. When they reached the bottom of the hillside on the north side, they would come to Bean Blossom Creek and the place where a few other settlers might have been seen at this point. The Creek was said to have been covered with bean sprouts which were flowering when it was discovered and thus named. This creek was large enough and wide enough they could have driven their wagons right across it without much problem. And, from that point northwards, their way would be less and less affected by the water courses and the little band could make much better time. There is another story about the naming of this creek but I'm not familiar with that. Today there is a covered bridge, recently refurbished, that was built in 1880 over this same creek. I have pictured it in this book.

I'll stop the history at this point in my narrative now. I have explained how some of them had to prepare foodstuffs and wagons, and themselves and their children to make this trek. I have been with this little band of people all the way from Corydon to their arrival in Brown County and then to their leaving it. Someone else will have to move them all the rest of the way to Indianapolis where they would live and spend their lives.

I hope you enjoyed our move northward, but this is who we are. Are you tough enough to have completed the trek northward?

PART TWO
THIS IS OUR BROWN COUNTY
1900-NOW

Embracing our Future

INTRODUCTION
TO PART TWO

The first part of this book was written to cover the historical years 1800-1900 specifically, but there will be showing some overlap in this next section with that first section simply because some of the history overlapped into the later years. For instance, in the first section I speak of the Bean Blossom covered bridge which was built in 1880 and is still in some use today. There are other instances you will notice that took part in more than one century, but I tried to point those places out as I typed the stories.

Other instances show up in the section that was written by my co-author Rhonda Dunn. In that instance there was the building of the Old Log Jail, the original courthouse building, and a few other areas. These were built in the 1800s but are still in use today, altered to fit the times and whether or not things were ever burned down such as the courthouse once was burned. Rhonda's recounting of how much has been preserved for our future is pretty comprehensive and I certainly appreciate her help in writing about our beautiful History Center, north of the present-day courthouse in Nashville where she is the archivist. If you ever need or want to know anything she can provide for you.

I also gave results from canning, preserving, pickling, hog killing time with the recipes as close to the real thing as I could remember what went into some, like the curing process. You will have to adjust them to your family's taste if you try to use them for your own preservation work. The drying methods I gave were the actual way we prepared fruit, beans, berries and other items to lessen the weight of them and make them long distance fresh if you kept them dry.

I mention the boarding houses and the arrival of our earlier artists in part one. Those people still come today and make up a large portion of our handcrafters and artists.

New in this section is the story of the chainsaw artists who are becoming popular here in Nashville and several other places that are intriguing to our visitors. Of course, I had to mention the candy and ice cream stores, our entertainment venues, and various other places you might like to visit.

With all this said, let's start this part of the book with our medical facilities which have grown greatly since my own time living here and I explain how I helped in this venture as well as with the placement of the Veteran's monument on the courthouse lawn and the free Thanksgiving dinner on Thanksgiving Day that has been going on now for 40 years.

Let's get started.

MEDICAL SERVICES

If you are visiting Brown County, or Nashville, or want to come here but are concerned about your health issues or disabilities and want to assure yourself that everything you use or need at home can be found here in Brown County, have no fears. We provide excellent health services now, but in the far past things were very different.

In the olden days of Brown County, if you were injured and needed care, or had a heart attack or fell on a sidewalk and broke your arm or leg, chances were good that any care you received would have been made by the one funeral home located in Brown County, then right here in Nashville. It has since moved to north of Nashville a mile or so.

There was no ambulance service and no emergency medical personnel, and it might have meant the funeral home and a staff member would be the one to take you to a hospital in their hearse to a nearby city for treatment. While we now have some medical services, there is still no hospitals or trauma centers yet today, but it has progressed far along the line into getting better health service.

Several years ago, I became an Emergency Medical Technician (EMT) and worked in an office in Nashville where it was possible for me to leave my office and go down the street and help someone with my hard-earned skills if no one else was available and the ambulance was already on an emergency run.

As I was kneeling over an older man one day after having taken his vital signs and talking him down a bit, this bearded guy wearing an old billed cap stopped by me, knelt down and asked about the man's vitals. I started to tell this man then thought better of doing that. Finally deciding what to answer, I asked this stranger, "Who are you and why are you interrupting me?" I asked him.

With a kind of smile on his face he introduced himself. "I am a doctor, and I am here to help you. I know you don't know me yet, but I am a new doctor in town," he responded. "I saw what you were doing as I looked out my window and thought to assist you if you needed my assistance."

Kind of red-faced at my faux pas, (social error) I allowed the new doctor to assess my patient. He concluded I was doing the right thing and advised me to call for an ambulance.

I was able to help not only this one patient, on a later day, I discovered another man in a rather awkward situation who was having chest pains but like a lot of men do, he was denying he was actually having a real heart attack. I am a very short woman, barely five foot tall, and learned that the man was camping at the local KOA Kampground inside a camper with the bed portion up over the cab of the truck.

In order to reach him, I had to step up on a dining chair, then onto the kitchen stove, and then pull myself up the rest of the way into the bed over the cab where my patient lay sweating and moaning, as I was myself by that time. I assessed him and told him he was having a heart attack, and asked others who had entered the camper after me for a back board and some straps. After securing the man to the backboard I then asked for four tall men to help me get him down off the bed and into the ambulance for a trip to a hospital to the east of Brown County. Then to help me get back off that bed and onto the floor.

A few days later I received a letter from this same man, who lived in Michigan, and was just recovering from having had to have open heart surgery, thanking me for being knowledgeable enough to recognize his symptoms for what they really were. "I think you may have saved my life," he told me. How wonderful it was to me to hear from a patient after I had assessed him correctly. I would spend several more years with the designation EMT on many accidents and sicknesses, and I enjoyed that part of my life immensely. I then got too busy in my career and let my license expire.

I, along with three prominent businessmen in Nashville, spent about 4 or 5 years trying to tempt either the Bloomington or Columbus Hospital to set up a small trauma center here in Brown County for just these kinds of cases so they could get prompt care to help stabilize them prior to being moved to the hospitals. This group failed in their efforts but when the local YMCA was built a few years later, both these hospitals placed an office and treatment center inside the YMCA just outside town in Salt Creek Park, so perhaps this group of hopeful, caring citizens did not fail after all.

Now Brown County has a fairly large cadre of well-trained first responders, EMT's, and proper ambulance service to any hospital in a surrounding county. We have a separate home for our ambulances and space for the EMTs to rest while they are on duty right next to the jail on State Road 46 right after the Brown County Inn complex. You may call 9-1-1 on your phone and they will come and help you or if you or someone responsible is driving your vehicle, you may pull into their location for immediate assistance.

We are equally blessed to have so many well-trained firefighters now also. In the past, medical training was secondary to other things if you were a firefighter. Now a large percentage of firefighters in our eight volunteer fire departments are trained EMTs or first responders as much so as they are for fighting fires. Their service is priceless to this small county.

They are a terrific group of people and well-trained for many emergencies. I can vouch for that. They have been to my home many times in the last four years since I have put a little age on my body and have taken to falling frequently, hurting myself many times. So far, I have broken both legs, one foot, one thumb and one shoulder and these guys were at my home every time to help me.

I fell in my home over a year ago during a really awful winter storm and ice was everywhere you stepped outside my home. About 14 first responders, firemen and EMTs and an ambulance were at my home within 20 minutes total.

After taking me to the hospital for my injuries to be treated, one of those who had responded to my call for help came back to my home while I was gone, shoveled the snow from my porch and steps and then had spread ice-melt all over the area so I would not fall again as I returned to my home. I have never read of this kind of selfless and thoughtful treatment in any county other than Brown County.

In addition to the presence of two hospitals with personnel in the YMCA, we have two or three eye care centers, an outstanding dentist, another doctor or two to assist you if you have problems while visiting us. So, we are moving right along with providing health care.

So be assured if you come to visit us, there are sufficient facilities for you to obtain needed health care.

Will you serve our community if you come here to live?

SALT CREEK PARK

The man who both owned and designed the Salt Creek Park shopping center was a good friend of mine. He respected my talents as much as I respected his ability to make his dream come true. His big dream was to create this shopping center, adding and leasing spaces for all those businesses he thought would help Brown County the most.

He, Roy Wininger, came to my real estate office after I opened that and would sit with his feet crossed and propped on my desk, facing me. I would sit across from him with my feet crossed and on my desk talking to him, sometimes for two hours or more. He thought it was perfectly natural to sit there and ask my advice for the types of businesses that should be placed out there. Me, a lowly peon and him a very wealthy, wise man, asking for and sometimes taking my advice.

I urged him at first to make sure the local IGA store was removed from town and taken out there, so that was the first building to go in, I believe, and it was prominently used to anchor the front Northwest line. That store remains our only grocery store here in Brown County. Then he added a branch bank and a savings and loan; a hardware store, and one fast food place which, after several name changes, is now a McDonalds. There are two motels, one is a chain, the other locally owned. The YMCA is there, as is the Bureau of Motor Vehicles and a laundromat. There are the other medical buildings and a carwash and the office of the Brown County Health Department.

Lastly there are two large three-story buildings each housing almost 200 or more elderly residents in small one- or two-bedroom apartments and a nursing home/rehab facility that I have used three times already. There are certainly more in this 40-acre field he had owned seemed like forever, but he projected our county's needs first of all, to make it the best place he could for our benefit. A terrific man.

Roy had asked me about the apartments for the elderly, debating whether his idea was a good one or not. I disagreed for once and suggested one building for the elderly and one for the younger families with children. One person in each building might want to connect with one in the other building; trade babysitting for driving chores, etc. I lost that debate but still think it was a good one. Perhaps I was wrong. I was told there was a four-year waiting list to get an apartment in either of the buildings. I give the floor to Roy on this one. In the very middle in the front of the property, that which started out as a drugstore, is now a Dollar General Store with several small stores surrounding the Dollar store on its two sides.

I think Roy had some terrific ideas for his property. He managed to entice the stores we use every day into this one area away from the busyness of the downtown area. We no longer have to fight the traffic to get through town to go to our courthouse or any other place we would have need to use on a daily basis.

I think it also shows that it doesn't matter if you are rich or not so rich, if you have an idea that you think will benefit the residents living here, there is someone who will listen to you and even sometimes take your advice.

This is just one way we are different here.

THOSE ELUSIVE MORELS

This is a sink full of mushrooms ready for the frying pan.

Well, the snow has melted, the floods have been and gone, mayapples are popping up and the grass is turning green. It must be getting about time for the morel mushroom season to begin for another year. You can always know it is their season when nearly every road you drive on will have several vehicles parked alongside the road, (legal or illegal, no one complains unless they are recently moved here city fellers.) You can see people walking in the brush and on the hillsides with their heads down looking at the ground. We natives understand exactly what they are doing. Without a doubt there is not a one out there who is not looking for these edible fungi. Everyone wants to find some morels.

Those elusive little buggers will be popping up everywhere in our little patch of woods within a few weeks or so and I want someone at this household to be ready to walk into those woods and pick us a bunch of them.

Morels are one of the first edible things that pop up in the springtime and nearly everyone I know hunts and eats them. They are extremely hard to find until your eyes become adjusted to the dimmer light now that winter is gone and leaves have started to bud out, forming a shady canopy, or until you spot your very first one.

After the first morel is found, it becomes a bit easier to find more. It takes a bunch of them to make a good mess (mess in this case is a withit to others.) And a withit is what you fix as a side dish when you already know what meat you will be cooking for supper (dinner is served at noon). We country folk call our evening meal supper while city folks call it dinner. Got it?

It takes about five or six messes to get your fill of the little fungi. After that it is a simple matter to dehydrate what fresh leftovers you may have, before you soak them in salt water to eat immediately.

Here's the recipe I use for that. I made this up but it really works from finding out through much trial and error. Cut each mushroom into two pieces lengthwise and hold each piece under the fairly gently running water of the faucet and let dry until they stop dripping. It is imperative that you not soak these fungi in salt water before you finish the procedure I give now. Once the mushrooms have been cut, washed and looked over for slugs and other bugs inside the stems of some, and dripped dry, they will be ready to eat or dehydrate.

BEWARE OF FALSE MORELS

Always make sure that you really have a mess of the real mushrooms as eating a false morel will give you more agony than you might want. In 2017 a neighbor who had eaten morels all his life, in error, got hold of a false morel and ate it. He ended up in the hospital for a while, critically ill and then was in the same nursing home I was in for rehab after my having had knee replacement surgery.

IDENTIFYING A FALSE MOREL

Because I had never seen a false morel, I asked him what to look for to make sure they are the real morel. He explained that the true morel has a hollow tube-like stem whereas a false morel has a solid stem. The tops look quite closely the same, so do please be careful. That is one reason you need to slice each morel in half <u>lengthwise</u>, while you are processing them preparing them to be eaten. It would be an easy way to tell the difference. If ever you are not sure which type of mushroom you have found, do not eat it. If there is a local expert you can show it to for identification, do so, because next time you will be able to identify it yourself.

Our late judge, my friend, Sam Rosen, wrote a book about mushrooms and gave pictures of the real thing to help those needing help to identify what was and was not edible. Sam loved to talk about mushrooms.

I bought an electric dehydrator through the newspaper want ads one year, or you can order one from Amazon or some other place, (a new one costs less than $100) and you can use it year after year for a long time. I have one that has seven trays you can do at one time. Space the pieces you wish to dehydrate on one of the trays, spaced close but not on top of other pieces. Set the temperature at 145 degrees and leave it there for about two-three hours before checking to see how they are doing. If they are dry and crisp, they are ready to finish. If you can still see or feel soft or damp spots, leave the morels in the dehydrator a bit longer and check before removing them just to make sure.

I either place them in a plastic ziplock bag and store them in my freezer, or otherwise, if you have a clean, white pillowcase, simply drop them in that and hang the whole shebang inside a closet. Then when the winter snow is flying again, take out as many as you think you will need. Get enough out for a good mess because remember now they are dehydrated, dry and very small in size. They will plump up later in this process.

When you want to have a mess in the wintertime, put the pieces in very salty warm water and let sit until they have become hydrated and back to their normal size once again. This might take two or more hours to completely reconstitute themselves. You may now rinse them through two or three rinses of cold water to remove the excess salt. Roll them in flour with a bit of pepper to taste and fry them in olive or canola oil until nice and brown. (Some fry morels in butter after rolling them in a flour and egg mixture). Remove them from the skillet and place each individual piece on a plate you have covered with paper towels to drain the excess fat. Eat and enjoy. Just don't eat too many and get a bellyache. You have to temper your stomach into certain new foods, and morels are one you must learn to do correctly.

I learned the hard way to not put them in salt water when I first started to preserve them. Salt makes them get mushy, turn black while rehydrating and you will ruin the whole batch.

Dehydration makes the morels taste as if they just came from the woods and I have tried everyone else's methods and to my taste, dehydration is best.

My husband and two sons were avid mushroom hunters and every year we seemed to have a plethora of them. So naturally, I always had some to eat now and some to eat when the next snow flies, but you can eat them at any time you like because it does not matter how long you store them.

My husband's favorite person to mushroom hunt with was named John Birdsong, a neighbor guy who lived nearby. John was never known to wear shoes, even in the briars or woods or snow. The soles of his feet had to be as tough as shoe leather to withstand this punishment. He was a really fun character to know.

My husband, Mickey, and sons, Lonnie and Douglas, would spend hours and hours in the woods every spring searching out these elusive fungi. I think it was not only the opportunity to walk in the spring sunshine and to catch up on conversations among the three of them. But more importantly it was to discuss these elusive fungi and how good they were going to taste when they were properly cooked at home.

It gave Mickey a familiar way of talking and giving his sage advice and was a good form of exercise and bonding with each other.

Lonnie and Mickey Ayers, 5 miles back in woods

When hunting mushrooms, they could spend nearly the whole day out in the hardwoods. Mickey and Doug knew every tree in the woods quite well and under which ones the morels were likely to be found. Mickey looked for older, rotten, or even falling down elm trees. Doug preferred sycamore trees and other types.

An incident happened one year when they were preparing to cross a small stream way back in the woods. There was a small tree that had fallen across the little stream they wanted to cross and as Lonnie prepared to step up on it Mickey saw the fallen tree "move."

It was not the tree moving, as it happened, but a large rattlesnake stretched out full length in the sun on that log. The snakes come out at about the same time as the morels do, so that is the other thing you might want to watch for when walking in our woods. My guys always carried a walking stick which they cut as soon as they got to the wooded area.

It not only helped them keep their balance and made walking easier but could be used as a probe to check for snakes. Both copperheads and rattlers are the only two poisonous snakes we have here in this county, but they are protected by law and you are not to kill them. But do try to avoid them. It helps some if the rattlers let loose with their songs of rapidly shaking the rattle area on the ends of their tails. Others that know say you can tell a snake's age by how many rattles it has on its tail. This helps you know for sure that snakes are near you. The copperhead snakes are not noisome so be careful. And, whatever you do, wear high top leather boots or shoes to protect yourself from snake bites. As I have noticed over the years, both snakes tend to stick their heads forward and then downward as they strike. We used to see them on a regular basis.

If you are bitten by a snake, try to find out what kind it was for the ER people to know how to treat you. If the snake is killed, check the eyes to see if the pupils are elliptical, (up and down, not rounded) and if they have a nostril on each side of their jaws. Of course both the copperhead and the rattler will have distinctive stripes or markings on its body.

Mickey and I were walking in the woods early one year before we thought the mushrooms would be up yet when I, frustrated at not finding one yet, and who had never found more than one or two in a hunt, yelled at him, "I wish one time in my life I could find a patch of mushrooms." Lordy, I was frustrated.

I was standing at the foot of an old rotten tree that had been down a long time and had nearly decayed away. I do not know to this day what kind of tree it was, but it had been probably three feet through, and I was not ready with a sack to bring any home with me if we did find some because it was so early in the season. Everyone who hunts them regularly will tell you to use a ventilated sack like potatoes come in and as you walk out of the woods with your loot the spores fall through the mesh and come back up the next year as morels.

Just happening to look down at my feet that day, I saw these fungi growing everywhere and yelled at him to bring me his tee shirt. I kept pulling the things and putting them in a pile. By the time he got to where I was standing there was a big pile.

I tied the arms and neck hole of his shirt with some vines I found and placed the morels inside his tee shirt, using it as a sack, until we got home. There were 104 morels in my pile!! For once I had gotten my wish. Now poison ivy, arthritis and other health problems keep me out of the woods.

One of the last times I ventured into the woods with the family I contracted the worst case of poison ivy I had had in my adulthood. It took 13 partial inoculations from my doctor to get rid of the rash and help my immune system prepare for the next time I got reckless. Nowadays I just stay out of the woods anymore. It just isn't worth the hassle to take a chance.

So, enjoy those precious morels, that if you had to purchase them, would cost you more than $30 or more per pound as we know since some people here follow the mushroom line clear up into Michigan and then donate the produce for a sale that benefits local charities.

Being able to find your way through unchartered territory to find the fungi and get back out of the woods is one major way we are who we are. I've been lost my entire life, so I always have had to go into the woods with a guide. My husband and sons were all like homing pigeons and were never lost.

Bon Appetit!!

Again, this is another way we are Brown County!! Bring your fully-charged iphone with the location app just in case you get lost as I do. And bring a light of some sort to alert helicopters of your location if you see one circling overhead or even a police-type whistle might come in handy. Sit down next to a tree and do not walk around in circles. Someone with better sense of direction besides me will find you eventually.

LIGHT POLLUTION

Here in Brown County might be where you want to live if you are a stargazer or if you are bothered by the smog in most of our cities and have breathing problems due to the smog. Sometimes in the cities we have visited the smell of the city is a pollutant. The cities always smell of burned potato chips.

It would be a rare day here in Brown County if you were enveloped in smog. We have no manufacturing businesses to produce the smog. Yup, nary a one. Our worst pollution would be the emissions from the millions of automobiles we have when the visitors arrive. A large majority of our male residents are self-employed in a variety of professions. It would be rare for them to be producing any noxious fumes to bother us. The ones who are not self-employed, work in other cities and commute.

We once had a sock-making factory located in Helmsburg, about 5 miles West from Nashville. Even though that factory made millions of pairs of socks every year, it was a non-polluting factory, unlike most factories which deal with many kinds of pollutants on a daily basis. But that kind of factory is unknown here. For some reason, a large part of the sock factory burned down and after repairing the building as best as it could be repaired after the fire so it could be sold, the factory owner moved it to Martinsville which is next county to our northwest and is prospering over there.

 We also once had a made-by-hand broom factory in Helmsburg and a train track running through that tiny town. Maybe witches needing a new broom, took that factory away, I'm not really sure. But it is now gone.

What we do have is pollution of another kind and that is light "noise" defined as not being able to see the stars and constellations at night as some would like to do, because so many yard lights at residences and businesses are pointed at the sky. The word "noise" is meant as a metaphor for the problem of its shining into the sky after dark which can disperse out of the place from where it is located.

Our youngest son, Douglas, who has written letters to the editor of the local newspaper, asked that yard lights be eliminated here. Barring the elimination of them altogether, perhaps requiring all these yard lights which are installed by local Rural Electric Corporations and cost a mere pittance each month on their electric bills, stop selling yard lights or replacing those already in existence with a light diffuser which directs all the light noise toward the ground instead of up in the air, essentially keeping it out of the sky.

Some, especially the elderly, may feel more secure with the yard lights shining outside their property so they can easily see what or who might be out in their yard causing the dogs to bark at night.

It really doesn't matter what the cause is other than light noise being a hinderance to being able to gaze up in the sky and see everything that happens up there. A lot of residents like to own and use power telescopes for that reason as we ourselves do. With so many lights pointing up at the sky you can see hardly anything of substance or even be able to identify someone on your property if you saw them walking outside your home and the police would ask you to identify a picture of an intruder. It is impossible to do so, therefore, why does everyone who moves to Brown County, or out in the country elsewhere, insist on having one of these lights in their yard? What good do they do? Or better yet, have your electric supplier remove yours or put a cover over the top of the light itself?

Whatever is done to prevent this type of pollution would be greatly appreciated by the stargazers in our population.

More and more larger cities are publishing rules against this pollution from the problems of bright lights that ruin the night sky.

Instead, why not get a smart dog to alert you to who might be outside your home? A smart dog that can tell you (if you listen closely) what it should be doing instead of just barking and keeping you and the neighbors awake.

A smart dog is different than just a plain old yard dog or a junk yard dog that barks at everything. A smart dog will have a bark that says there is someone or something they do not know outside your home. If they are growling or barking furiously it might mean that someone they do not recognize is out there and they are up to no good.

Their instincts are rarely wrong so pay attention to them when they talk to you.

If your pet is not a smart dog it would behoove you to go to the nearest Humane Society and find one. I'm sure that every animal shelter in the country has a dog or two they would be glad to send to a home here in Brown County as long as your place is appropriate for the pet you want. Not merely a pet as such but maybe as a defender of your property and is very smart to boot.

We recently completed a long-awaited project here in this county of building a new animal shelter. (See picture above.) It is far larger than the small one we had used for several years. It is open now to the public. We take care of our pets and have them spayed and neutered for better control of the animal population. And since you live in the country now, you need to make sure your pets are up-to-date on their vaccinations. This is important.

I hope Brown County can lead the way in this endeavor to stop the light noise and to place our animals in responsible homes once they leave our beautiful animal shelter.

That makes us a special sort of people doesn't it? Won't you join us?

SONG AND DANCE

For many years, I'm talking here from about 1935 up into the present day, Brown County has had a surplus of venues which are today referred to as song and dance places. After all, many of the settlers in Brown County came from the hills of Appalachia, or across the Ohio River and then when they got to Brown County, they saw a place very much like the one they had just left, and said, "This is it. We are here. This is home."

They saw the hills, for sure smaller than the mountains they had left behind them in the eastern states and loaded with virgin timber, which they had all seen before, and realized that here was where they wanted to settle, to live and to die, so settle they did. A lot of their descendants are still alive here today, many living the lifestyles they learned as youngsters from their parents.

In the earliest days of Brown County most of the residents lived a very rough life. They held barn raisings and building small log homes, raising chickens and hogs for their meat and eggs, fishing from our streams, and teaching their youngsters those same rules they themselves had been taught down in Appalachia's mountains.

Today there are about 15,000 souls residing in this paradise we all love but are willing to share with outlanders or "furriners" as some would call them, who come to visit and then some decide to stay, build a log cabin on a bit of acreage, and send their children to a modern, but much smaller school for their learning pleasure.

We have three elementary schools, an intermediate school, a junior high and a high school. All have good reports when tested and rated by the state.

I have lived here for more than sixty years now and would not want to return to any other way of life. I'm just not sure I could survive elsewhere. My knowing so many people who live here from my days of managing the local Brown County Democrat newspaper I have found my long-time and forever home, I hope. I'm like a stray dog that finally finds it "furever" home. I'm here to stay.

I have known and loved so many of the older people who lived and died here and have heard so many of their stories that have stuck with me much of my years here that I would like to tell you about their musical beginnings.

At one time there was a well-known and well-visited IGA grocery store in Bean Blossom, (the grocery no longer exists, and the store has been sold to a Dollar Store). Bean Blossom lies just about 5 miles north of Nashville that had another building right next to the regular grocery store just begging for someone to use that small building. Way back when, probably 1930s or a bit later, before my time, someone did. At least several people from Van Buren Township answered the call, formed a country band, and played music there on the weekends.

The band members were Hesper "Hep" Anthony Beauchamp and her husband Adolph "Doc" along with Hep's sister, Wilma Anthony Spiker, and Louis Henderson along with his wife, Mabel, started going up there from their homes in Van Buren Township and playing music and singing their hearts out. I don't believe Mabel played music but her husband Louis never left home without her. If you saw one, you saw both, that was just the way it was with this couple, whether at their own farm or out in public.

Those wishing to dance could do so on the concrete parking lot of the grocery store, or on state road 135 itself if the traffic was light enough and at that time in our history, the road was probably safe enough.

I remember a funny story about the Hendersons. They loved big Buick cars for more than one reason. They were always seen together, and their big cars were not merely for their transportation if they needed to go somewhere, they were also used as a farm "tool." If they had a big sow or two to move somewhere else, they would put it in the back seat area and take it there. When one of these Buicks wore completely out, and the fenders and bumpers flopped when the car moved, they would call the local junkyard and tell the owner (Clinton Cooley) to come get the old one and bring them a new Buick. Or if they were on their tractor moving around the farm for some reason, Louis would be driving the tractor and Mable would be standing on the rear draw bar with her arms around Louis's belly holding on for dear life. This childless couple was completely dedicated to one another. It was amazing.

This little band continued this venue of old-time country music for many years before age caught up with them and they retired. Another group of people kept the venue going as long as they could and by then they had heard that Bluegrass Hall of Famer, Bill Monroe, had bought a few acres of ground almost across the road from the old venue.

Even though Bill Monroe and his band were Bluegrass musicians, they were welcomed to the area and that place became very popular. Today the Bill Monroe Bluegrass Park still exists and is well patronized by many visitors from several states. It hosts many festivals each year, and has added a museum, parking lot, camping and mini storage areas to the park.

From its rustic wooden stage and plank seating, or if you had brought your own lawn chair, you could spend hours and hours with your ears attuned to this nostalgic type of music. This was the true music of the Appalachia Mountains where I was born and spent six years of my life before moving to Jackson County to a farm in Kurtz, and where many of our residents had come from.

For about 25 years or more, there was the Little Nashville Opry, just west of Nashville a half mile or

so. It provided a modern building and stage for famous country singers from the A-List of country music every Saturday night. On Friday nights it gave way to local musicians that was led by one of the owners. Their own house band was terrific as I went to several of their shows and can vouch for it.

That was one of the most popular venues in the Midwest if you wanted to hear true country music. It was popular with both the natives and industry greats. Unfortunately, after a show many years ago now, it burned to the ground. Police called it arson, but no one ever stood trial for that crime. We will never know now if it was arson as both the owner/operators are now deceased.

It took several years before Brown County decided to build its own music center. It is now complete, and the Brown County Music Center is located on the first street to the south after you pass the Salt Creek Park shopping area on State Road 46 East. It was built using Brown County tax dollars, so it is ours. If you look to the west in their parking lot you will see the Brown County Health and Living nursing home or you might see a whole herd of beautiful, sleek, black and white cattle strolling by the venue to go to pasture each morning or home to the barn for the evening. Their owner rents pasturage from available farms and runs his young cows on this pasturage. It is rumored he has over

500 head of these cattle, some at his home farm and others in these small, rented pastures. A different kind of farming.

I would suggest you make reservations and buy your tickets well in advance to see shows at the Brown County Music Center (Brown County's gift to itself) as it has become a nice draw and through its tax status, benefits the residents of this county very nicely. After the Covid-19 illness passed, this venue picked back up again. At one time it was being used for the immunization and testing for Covid-19 and has since been changed back to its original purpose.

For awhile, we had another music venue. The old Bond funeral home building was purchased by a couple who opened a cabaret type show which was very popular. Since the funeral home had a new building north of Nashville on State Road 135, this couple chose the name of "Pine Box Theater," and everyone loved the name with its obvious nod to the funeral home. This venue was up and running about a dozen or more years and was very popular but when one of the owners passed away, this venue closed, and it now houses the Salvation Army.

There are several places in Brown County where you can hear music if you want to visit and eat dinner, and some have live music at times. But the ones I have mentioned in this book are the ones I know more about and the others may change bands frequently.

For the dance part of this story, we will talk about a dance venue just West of Nashville, over the big hill. At the bottom of the hill on your left you will see a huge barn, called Mike's Dance Barn.

On some Saturday nights it is usually packed with about 75 dancers who love to line dance to live music from the stage. Mike Robertson is the owner and is a mean player on the yakkety sax. Mike is about as good as you will hear anywhere. My son, Douglas, loves to go there and mingle with his many friends. On Monday nights they give dance lessons. There is a small fee to enter, and good food comes out of their kitchen for those who are hungry and need to eat and rest. It is normal for these dances to go on for 45 or more minutes at a time, so a rest period is a blessing.

I have decided that if my arthritis wasn't so bad, this would be a good way of getting therapy at a cheap rate instead of going to my doctor. But alas, old Arthur is getting the best of me. I guess I waited too long.

One of the early venues located right on Van Buren Street in Nashville, is the Brown County Playhouse. It is now owned by this county and provides occasional movies, plays, cabaret and other ways of enjoying oneself. This venue was once owned by Indiana University. The schedule varies but goes on for much of each year.

So, if you want good music and want to do a vigorous dance, come to Brown County and join us.

You are all invited to learn how to be Brown County

BROWN COUNTY'S "WILD" LIFE

When I am speaking of Brown County's "wild" life I am not speaking about its speakeasies or taverns or things like that. In fact, I don't know of any tavern in Brown County nowadays. There are taste testing places at some of the wineries, and in other places that serve food with a drink, but no taverns as such, with the closing of the Pine Room Tavern.

The Pine Room had been a landmark for many, many years. It was one of those places where you could stop after work, still wearing your old work clothing and dirty boots to have a cold one. I am speaking of its actual wildlife, animals of which we have so many and a good variety of them.

As I grew up in another state and then a county other than Brown County, my family never saw the abundance of wild animals that I began seeing when I married and moved to Brown County. I cannot recall ever seeing one much less an abundance of them until I actually moved here to begin my married life in Story.

All around that tiny town you could drive around at night and see literally scores of deer in every field you passed. It was illegal to spotlight them, but in order to count them you had to use a light, and besides that my husband enjoyed showing off this wildlife to me as much as he knew I loved seeing it.

I guess the conservation officers might have taken your word for it if they saw you spotting the deer if you did not have a gun in your car and it was just my husband showing me the fields full to overflowing with these magnificent creatures. But they never stopped us once to check us out and we became acquainted with all of the Conservation Officers (COs) in those days. But when deer season started, at the first sound of a gunshot, every deer in every field, would flee to the Brown County State Park which was off limits to hunting.

In Jackson County to the south of Brown County where I grew up for about 10 years of my life and never saw even one deer, it is now deluged with them. There are so many farmers down there who plant grain that it is much easier for the deer to find something to eat, and they are much larger than those here in Brown County which has lost a lot of its farmers.

On two separate occasions last year I watched as two of these lovely creatures gave birth to their babies as I sat on a stool washing our dishes and watched out the window. How often have you even thought of seeing this event? I have now seen this only four times in 60 years. It is a privilege to me to see nature at its best.

Another time, Mickey and I were in our garden, hoeing the tomatoes and we heard one of our two beagle dogs, Beau, barking like crazy. We looked up and saw Beau running right toward us with a mama deer right on his tail kicking up dirt behind itself. The dog reached us and, crouching and shuddering, it then hid completely behind Mickey's legs so the deer could not see any part of him. The mama deer finally looked up and saw both of us standing there with our hoes in our hands and came to a halt, maybe thinking we were holding guns. It had to have also been thinking "where did it go."

We figured the dog had gotten too close to its baby and the mama was just taking care of its own.

Then there were the masked bandits in the Brown County State Park. By that I mean we saw raccoons by the dozens, mostly climbing into every trash barrel in the park looking for leftover food, strewing food and trash all around every barrel.

Nowadays you cannot put anything in a trash barrel in the park because they were all removed several years ago to deter this mischievous creature. You are asked to bring trash bags into the park when you visit or pick up one at the gatehouse as you check in and take all trash out with you when you leave that you had brought into the park.

These little guys are such fun to watch. I have a funny story about one. My husband, Mickey, heard something on our back deck early in the night a long time ago. I always kept a locking plastic trash barrel on that porch which held our dog's food. When

Mickey went onto the porch and turned the overhead light on, the lid was off the barrel of food and down on the floor.

Somehow that little rascal had used its paws to turn the lid enough he could unlock the lid and had climbed down into the kibble. As Mickey looked down that cheeky little guy was pushing food into his own mouth with one paw and offered Mickey a bit of kibble with the other front paw, as if to say, "Have a piece, I have lots of it here." But Mickey, in his gruff voice, told the little bandit to get out of there and after it did so, he relocked the food barrel, deterring the raccoon for the rest of the night at least.

About ten years ago we started seeing millions of sandhill cranes down in the Brownstown/Ewing bottoms. (Long after our travelers went through there.) Every spring they came there on their way north and every fall they came there again to head south where they would migrate for the winter.

While Mickey was outside one day, he heard the call the birds made and saw the sky was nearly dark with those birds high overhead. We have been on their flyway ever since and notice them flying both north and south.

During this past week, a friend and I drove down to see how things were going with the cranes. Most of them had already flown North and left the bottoms where they stood in standing water overnight. The White River had overflowed its banks and left little indentations across hundreds of acres and that was exactly why they were there. The water, I read one year, was their protection so they stood in that water most of the time they were in our area. I have often wondered how they protect their feet when the water ices over.

Their food, which they ate constantly, was the dropped grains of corn or soybeans left there when the local farmers harvested their crops the previous year and the water had softened it. After a good feed-up of a couple of weeks or longer, you would see them start their next leg of the northern flight where they mate and raise their young, or south to their breeding grounds.

These birds are a good predictor of our coming weather. If they stay here longer, it means it is still too cold up north for them to begin nesting, so they keep feeding and stay a while yet.

In earlier years, we had never once seen a congregation of birds like these gangly, stilt-legged birds in our area, now they are very common. No one seems to know why their flight pattern has changed, but it definitely has. Ten years or less ago, you would not have witnessed the millions that might congregate in Jackson County. I have seen numerous 1000-acre fields totally white with their plumage as they wait near Brownstown. A magnificent sight to say the least. They are mostly white looking on the ground, but if way high in sky look really dark.

When the cranes are in the air those long stilty legs protrude backwards and act as their rudders. Their voices sound like someone gargling. We have learned a lot about these birds. Mickey always thought there was something special about our ground here on our farm such as something magnetic which made them circle around and around over our place then when they got everything straightened out again, they chose a new leader and then would fly away. Our son, Douglas, came up with a better idea when he saw them this year. He said they were circling to gain height by flying on a thermal wind. That makes more sense to me.

Once upon a time we saw thousands of Canadian geese everywhere, but in the winter they would migrate. Today they are permanent residents here and in surrounding counties and they no longer migrate. Their migration patterns, like the sandhill

cranes, have also altered for some reason.

Other wildlife we often see are `possums, coyotes, wild turkeys, and many other lesser critters. Mickey happened to be looking out our dining room door one day about two years ago and saw a coyote take a flying leap and jump over our deck rail which would have been about a six-foot upwards jump. Seeing

Mickey's cat where it lived on our deck, it immediately grabbed it in its mouth, made a quick U-turn and went back over the high deck rail with the cat in its mouth.

It got a rude awakening when Mickey hollered at it to "Let my cat go." When the coyote's feet hit the hard ground outside the deck, it jarred the cat loose and it immediately ran up the big maple tree which stands there and went as high up as it could go. It took three days of trying to coax the cat down out of the tree, but it finally came back down.

We usually hear the coyotes with their shrill barking, much like a dog's bark only shriller, in the hardwoods behind our house every spring I expect during the birthing of their babies.

It isn't only cats the coyotes bother, it includes dogs also. Another time we arrived home to find a coyote was mating with our coon dog up by our barn. Now most people say that animals will not mate with anything of another species, but this one did, probably because they are so closely related as a species, and we got nine of the most beautiful puppies in a short while and kept one which turned out to be one of the strongest dogs I have ever known.

` Possums, or if you want to be exact, opossums, like to tease dogs. One day I was looking out my front door to see what the dog was barking so long about and saw it was a `possum "playing `possum" by pretending it was dead, just beyond the front door. That dog used its snout and tried valiantly to get it to move so it could grab it and that little beggar never moved an inch. Wherever the dog pushed it, that's where it lay, completely motionless, almost like it really was dead. At least it convinced the dog it was. City folk may have never seen this happen or have even heard of it happening, but I have seen it several times.

About half an hour later it seemed to realize that the dog had gone away, and it took it so long to look around to check for sure by turning its head that it was almost impossible for me to see the move. Once the `possum realized the dog had gone, it hopped up and took off like lightening to the nether regions of the hardwoods behind the house.

Another time one very young `possum got into the first branch of a small sumac tree next to our basement patio. It had evidently been there for some time when I arrived home because the dogs were exhausted and almost foaming at the mouth from barking at it so long. The dog could not reach to that first tree branch to molest it. It was just a young `possum and it would look down at the dogs and swish that ratty tail and I still think it was laughing at the dogs.

Just last week, Douglas was looking out our big dining room window and ran into the living room and told me to be quiet, and to come and see what he saw. For the first time in a very long time, we counted 36 turkey hens walking very sedately across the yard. There were several, most of which came from the wooded area as the tail end of the first batch went into the north side of the woods so we could not keep track of exactly how many we saw. In the past we might see 15 or 20 hens but never this many. He made a video to prove it.

When I became disabled after having back surgery and then developing sepsis in the early 1990's, I went to the big 10-acre lake across the road from our home and fished in it nearly every pretty day. I was sitting on a big rock that jutted out of the ground near a small cove, catching a lot of bluegill fish when I saw a large shadow fly over my head which seemed so low overhead, I ducked to avoid it. This magnificent bird landed in a dead tree snag on the other side of the cove which was at most 20 feet over to it. From its perch there it started screaming at me scolding me for being in its feeding grounds. It was the most beautiful bald eagle I had ever seen in the wild and up that close.

I let it screech at me for a time, then pulled my equipment out of the water and left the magnificent bird to its own hunting foray. We occasionally see these birds closer to our home now since the conservation department built nests for them to use down at Lake Monroe which, as the crow flies, isn't that far away from us. The eagles are making a real comeback because of this bit of help from the COs.

That same nearby lake is a popular place to see scores of wild geese on the ground. I was there fishing again at another time, and I could hear birds flying toward the lake and turned to watch them. There were three geese in that bunch, and they were dedicated to stopping at this lake and doing their own fishing. The gaggle of geese on the ground did not like these three; I think because we have always been told that geese mate for life and here was a gander with two mates, which made the other geese on the ground become alert and nervous.

The minute the three landed on the water, all the other ganders on the ground went out to try to run these three off, but the new gander held his ground. He literally walked on water then would flap his wings in their faces then swim off really quickly to get away from the others. They swam over a good portion of that ten-acre lake, fighting like mad with those geese on the ground.

It was so amazing I had to stay and watch what would happen next. After about 15 minutes, the mates to the gander went out to assist him and helped get him away from the unfriendly geese on the ground who were now on the water chasing after him, but eventually the three newcomers gave up and lifted off the water. I had just witnessed a miracle I think. I had never seen a goose (or anything else for that matter) actually walk on water, but today I had.

In Nashville on an errand with Douglas last week he told me about a shop in Antique Alley that had intrigued him. The artist, using no oils or watercolors as most artists use, was producing animals from the woods by using a chainsaw atop a large stump, creating these creatures and they were so life-like that it was amazing. The remainder of the uncarved stump would become its stele, or base, I suppose. So, if you are ever visiting our fair town, take a short stroll into the Antique Alley and see another type of artist perhaps at work that I am telling you about. I would love to have one of his carvings in my front yard or on my deck. There's more to art than oils and easels here in Brown County. This guy was a true artist.

We feed the birds in winter to try to save as many of them as we can with seed and suet and see so many species of these beautiful of God's creatures it is a real pleasure to see and help them. A salt block is usually standing out in our field so I can watch for the deer who come up and lick either the block itself or, after the salt has melted into the ground, they will lick that also. We also maintain a small stack of hay to feed the deer in winter and a feeder we fill with shelled corn which spits out just so many kernels at a time which help keep both the deer and the turkeys from being destroyed in a heavily snowy winter.

We never shoot anything nor allow other hunters on our property anymore, especially bird hunters. For about three years in a row, I had what I always referred to as a demented quail. It would stand out in the field and say "Bob" but could never say the second word "White." It has been a while since I heard this one, so I have to assume it is now deceased.

Another bird we hardly ever hear anymore is the lowly "Whip Poor Will". Many years ago, I was on the phone to New Jersey talking with my oldest brother when one of these guys sat out on the back deck rail and sang its song. My brother, Palmer, asked me to please stick the phone outside the sliding door and let him hear the bird sing, so I did. He said he had not heard a Whip Poor Will since we left Kentucky in 1948. So here I am paying long distance charges to let my big brother get one of his wishes.

Crows have taken over our farm. Some of them nest about 400 yards from our house and we have just about given up on them. But when we have a garden growing nicely and are about ready to harvest our sweet corn, they are real pests, but we also keep an old skillet outside and even feed these black cawing birds. They have to eat too, I guess, so we do that much for them. They are about the size of a bantam chicken now and I'm always surprised since they are so big that they can rise from the ground and fly away to their treetop nest, but they manage.

I even suggested to Mickey one time that we go to a laundromat and get their box of unmatched socks and slip one over every ear of sweet corn in his garden, but he never wanted to do that. It seemed like a good solution to me.

I will mention snakes again before I stop this little vignette. Yes, we have snakes here, rattlesnakes and copperhead snakes, which are the only poisonous ones that can bite you, but we have others that are not poisonous but maybe if one takes your big toe into its mouth, it can scratch around on you a bit. If you are smart, you will give them all their own space.

Do not try to catch one with your bare hands, even on a dare. And whatever else you do, do not crawl back into a ground cavity head-first (one person tried this) and try to get one. You might come back out without a nose. And never reach into a woodpile in the park or any other camping area without looking first to check for these snakes. Both species are protected by law.

I had two sisters who were so petrified of snakes they screamed at the very mention of or even on seeing pictures of snakes. I, on the other hand, give them a wide berth and let them go their way while I go mine. As long as I know they are there, I feel safe. My greatest fear though, is for something much smaller; BUGS! Especially June bugs or any other type of creepy crawlie or even the lowly worm.

I fainted more times than I can count when I was young and my older sister put a June Bug down the back of my dress.

When we first moved here to the farm from down in Story, the only place I could make a garden that first year was the round circles made when Mickey burned trashy trees and brush as he cleared space for our new home.

I was picking the last of the small round peppers to chop and freeze for soups when a tomato or tobacco worm (they both look the same to me) got on one of my fingers and stayed there until I went screaming and hollering into the house and told Mickey to remove the ugly thing. His reply was, "If you will go into a cobra cage over at Nashville and take a picture of a pile of 75 cobras, I'm not getting a worm off your finger." (I really had done that very thing one time for the newspaper). I held that against him a long time and I never picked another pepper that whole year. So there. I was no Peter Piper.

So, when I speak of wildlife, it's these animals and birds and such that are about as wild as it gets at our house. Hope you enjoy these little vignettes about our wild "wildlife".

Just another thing that makes us Brown County.

LITTLE COUNTRY STORES

At one time, in years long gone, there was literally a small Mom and Pop store in nearly every little burg that contained a half dozen or so homesteads. But Brown County lost much of that nostalgia ten or more years ago when most shoppers started enjoying going to the larger big box stores or those nice ones in the strip malls of nearby cities. Today, there are only a handful of those older types of stores still left, and none in this area.

The storekeepers/owners were usually the only employees, sometimes, perhaps helped by one or more of their own children. You could find almost everything you wanted, but you might be required to pay a few pennies more for an item than you would have had to pay if you had gone to a larger city to purchase something.

But the convenience of being able to run into a Mom and Pop and be waited on by someone who knew you personally and most likely knew every one of your children too, or could have guessed ahead of time what it was you wanted, is sorely missed in today's fast-paced world.

One store near my home was run by a man and wife who had started out selling hay and other animal feeds in a tiny shed across from their home years prior to my knowing them. They did so well selling hay and such from this shed that they then built a regular store across the road on property they owned then did a landslide business for as long as it was open. Others did not fare as well.

This store not only carried grocery items, but the "Mom" owner (Norma Crouch) also served simple hot sandwiches or hot soups or chili cooked daily for those needing to eat. Most likely, they would be senior citizens or workers on their lunch break. The "Pop" part (Harry Crouch) carried plumbing supplies to keep you from having to drive the 15 miles to the city to buy a tiny item that may have cost $.25 cents, and it still carried animal feed and tons of other things every homeowner needed.

The Mom of this operation had picnic tables both inside and outside the store where you could sit and talk to others like yourself, or who just needed an item or two or saw someone they had been wanting to kibitz with and then sat and talked a spell.

To help the hunters who came there to check-in their deer or turkey kills, she took care of that as well as took pictures of the hunters with their prize kills and sent the pictures to the local newspaper and put a copy of the picture on one of her large bulletin boards inside the store which after a few years contained hundreds of pictures. Some of these hunters came from 50 miles away just to check their deer kills at this little store. They loved this act of kindness.

To entice the younger crowd to come inside, there were pool tables where they could hone their skills. One rather small feller would come swaggering inside after supper with his personally purchased cue stick to play for a while. He was the only one to bring in his prize cue stick he had ordered, and was so proud of, to tempt the older boys into playing against him. A fairly good pool shooter for his small size, it was easy for him to play dumb and beat the tar out of the bigger guys. His reward was the bigger guys had to pay the quarter for him to play the next game, then he would just swagger back out of the store and go home.

That store is no longer open. Neither are the stores in other areas of the county. One or two have become classy restaurants while others were either just shuttered and the buildings removed or left vacant. For whatever reason and how and why it happened, all the little grocery stores, which we locals call Mom and Pops, are now a thing of the past.

An elderly man I interviewed for the local newspaper who lived in that area I was telling you about was very tiny. He related the story to me about a pair of shoes he had been trying to break in so the leather might soften up. Returning inside his home he brought out the still shiny shoes he had told me about. He had kept them polished and shined and sitting on his fireplace mantel. Bought many years ago at another nearby Mom and Pop store, I had to ask him how many years he had been trying to soften that leather and he replied, "50 years." He had bought them from a local Mom (there was no Pop) back when he was a young man.

When the Mom of that store finally married her boyfriend of 48 years and closed the store, it was sold and eventually became a fancy restaurant in this old run-down rusty metal building. Another story he told me was that when he was called to be inducted into the Army, he went there and this is what they told him. "Go back home and grow a little, we don't have uniforms that small." By this time, I was intrigued by what he was telling me. I asked him how big he had been at that time, and he told me he had weighed 86 pounds, so he went back home but now in his 80s he still weighed the same and was just about my own five foot height.

 This is the type of conversation that makes life in Brown County so wonderful. You could almost name everyone you saw and a lot of these conversations took place in one of these small community Mom and Pop stores. Most of the time you knew the news long before it was printed in the local weekly newspaper just by visiting one of our Mom and Pop stores. But about 10 years ago, something changed. I'm not sure what it was that stripped this type of store of its aura. Maybe the big box stores or the strip mall stores caused it, I do not know. I do know that between State Road 46 East to State Road 135 South, all the way down through 3 or more entire townships in Brown and Jackson County, and beyond State Road 50 for a good ways, there was not one single place left where you could stop and buy a simple loaf of bread or a stick of gum. People living where we do would have to drive 50 miles round trip to pick up a gallon of milk or anything else. It was a real hardship on many.

Update: A new Dollar General Store recently was built and opened along State Road 135 in Freetown, which lies south of Van Buren Township in Brown County. My husband went inside to purchase a couple of items we needed and to look over the new store right after its opening. He came out with a handful of items. At that point I urged him to go back inside and tell them they might consider offering bread and milk and such.

When he went back inside to tell them my idea, the clerk took his arm and walked him to a part of the store which showed him not only those items but a fairly large section containing frozen and fresh foods. What a blessing that was to so many. It cuts off about 20 miles driving each way for us to go to a grocery store in Jackson County. Now, if they would just add a corner eatery it would be great. **Update:** That eatery is now open for business and is located only three blocks from the Dollar Store. It is located in a building once housing, you guessed it, a Mom and Pop grocery store and serves excellent food.

There was a general store in Story, Indiana, where my husband's family, and we ourselves lived for 20 years after our marriage, and from where that pair of shoes for the elderly man had been purchased. It has been turned into a gourmet restaurant and wine tasting venue. They eventually bought the entire little town except for one home and turned it into an exclusive Bed and Breakfast.

Some other little grocery stores have been maintained in other parts of Brown County. Some are still regular little eateries or carry a few groceries. At least one in a town that doesn't even have a sign to designate its name, began life in an old dilapidated but renovated farmhouse and now serves wonderful fresh entrees and salads and sandwiches.

Another, Gatesville store, was torn down and a new one built across the road and is a popular place to grab a bite to eat. This store carries a variety of pans for those wishing to pan for gold in nearby Salt Creek. Gnaw Bone has space for gas, groceries and fast food cooked on the premises. (Don't you love some of our town names? I do.)

The loss of these Mom and Pops are a sore loss to this rural county that now has only one grocery store. Now not every place you walk into, even though you may have lived in Brown County all your life, there probably won't be a soul inside who can call you by your own name.

Farewell old friends. This too is Brown County

SHOPPING

It is estimated that there are 300 stores and restaurants in Nashville, each offering food, art, gifts, homemade crafts, and many other things of interest to Nashville's visitors.

Until about 20 years or so ago, almost every shop in the town of Nashville was a log cabin which had been repurposed into a store selling wonderful things.

Now there are quite a few of these shops residing inside big three-story buildings so don't overlook going into each store in each of the bigger structures if you want to see all of what Nashville has to offer in the way of gifts.

Almost any type of gift can be picked up while you visit in Nashville or if you make a note of which store had something you wanted to purchase, it is easy to do the shopping in the comfort of your own home.

While in the stores, ask if they have a free copy of "The Brown County Almanack" or "Our Brown County" magazines. Make a note on each of the ads appearing in these booklets that you want to buy after you go home but don't want to buy and have to tote it around town while you are still eating or browsing. Many of the stores will mail you whatever you have ordered and paid for while you are in their shop so you don't have to tote gifts around town. Just pay the store for that convenience.

Or once home, open the booklets to pages you have marked and go to this website where anything you want can be ordered shipped to your front door. Simple and easy isn't it.

BrownCountysouvenir.com is the place that can provide you with a nice gift for anyone in your family or circle of friends.

But while in town, stop by and feast on the many items these wonderful chefs have cooked up for you. And all the candy shops will usually have sample platters with small pieces of their wares you can put on your tongue and savor the taste before you buy more of that particular kind by the pound. One candy store used to advertise how many different licorice flavors they had, and they sold lots of different flavors, all made right there in their shop. There are lots of candy and ice cream stores located all across town. I must have gained 20 pounds over the 21 years I worked at the newspaper office and had to go to the post office for our mail by stopping at each of the candy stores and sampling their candies. For one of my free Thanksgiving dinners served on Thanksgiving Day, one of these candy stores donated 40 pounds of candy for me to distribute to the children attending the dinners. What a great show of kindness by these proprietors.

Another shop donated over 700 pieces of Christmas tree decorations for me to use at these dinners, and Santa Claus in full regalia made an appearance at each dinner.

If you are about to expire for want of a good cup of coffee, there are several types available on Van Buren Street.

If you don't want to stand in line and wait for your name to appear on a reservation chart at the larger restaurants, there are numerous places where you can pick up something simple like quarter pound hot dogs, gyros, popcorn, etc. Just step up and order.

Nashville today is far different than it was for our early settlers who had to bathe in the nearby Salt Creek and sleep in their wagons on their northern trip to Indianapolis. There is a striking difference between then and now.

You can buy nearly anything from toys, food, gifts, leather items, tee shirts or balsamic vinegar or the candy and Ice cream. Surely there is something you desperately need and want. If so, you can find it in uniquely wonderful, Nashville, Brown County, Indiana.

For 21 years I was the general manager of the Brown County Democrat newspaper, the only newspaper published in Brown County, and frequently rated the blue-ribbon newspaper in Indiana, and for those 21 years, I was one of the main writers and producers of this newspaper.

I cannot think of anyone else besides myself, who knew and wrote about so many people living in our back water county. I was one of those kinds of people everyone said they "knew" even though they were not personally acquainted with me. They maybe knew "of me" because either my picture or name appeared in almost every issue of that newspaper. This still happens to me. I was in the nursing home after some serious surgery recently for rehab and I felt I knew about half the residents and a goodly number of the staff, but, of course, I was like they were, I "knew" them through seeing their names in the newspaper or hearing strangers talking to me about some of them. It gives you a good warm feeling to know the majority of friends I made during my working years still "know" me.

I loved to go out into the county, meet strangers in their own homes and come back to the office and write wonderful stories of those same people. So many of these strangers later became my friend for life.

I received a phone call one time from an elderly woman who had not received her newspaper and she told me I should bring her one to her home on my way home. "I knew your grandparents, and they would want you to do this," she advised me. I agreed to stop by her home. The couple she thought were my grandparents actually belonged to my husband but that made no difference to Edna or to me.

When I got there her husband, Charlie, had picked me about a peck of fresh green beans from their garden, along with pulling me some green onions and a big garlic bulb. Since they were being so kindly Edna asked Charlie to go back out there and dig me some fresh new potatoes. "Helen can't have fresh green beans without also having some new potatoes with them," Edna told Charlie. This made sense to all three of us and I got a large bunch of new potatoes which are different from the ones left in the ground until harvest. When I left their home, the whole backseat of my car was loaded. Other stops would see me having to try a piece of his pies. The wife had had a stroke and the husband had to take over the cooking chores.

Another older couple lived in Helmsburg and had a farm on a hill overlooking that tiny town. The couple both attended the Indianapolis Farm Market every week, selling produce from their fairly big farm or things like eggs they purchased locally and took up there. They both were delightful people and had been selling in Indianapolis for several years.

One or the other would call me at the newspaper and speak to no one but me and put an ad in for that week to tell what produce they would have for sale and ask me to stop by the farm and they would pay me in cash, so I did. One week in the fall Glen put an ad in for fresh turnips. I asked if he had a lot of them, and he replied he had about ten acres, and he wasn't kidding. When I stopped it looked like a green ocean blowing in the wind.

My husband had been attending the Indiana Police Academy early one summer and was due home in three days. I stopped to talk to Glen to see if he had sweet corn yet and ended up surprised. He had been on his tractor in the garden, cultivating his tomatoes. When he saw me he immediately turned the tractor toward me and came and gave me everything I was wanting to cook for Mickey's welcome home meal. The next week when I stopped to pick up their ad money, his wife, Mary, came outside and told me not to go to the garden area. "Last week he plowed up half our tomatoes when he saw you," she told me as she shook her finger at me. I laughed for hours over that one. They were wonderful friends but so elderly at that time I'm sure they are long gone now. I miss seeing and talking to these kinds of elderly.

In 2017 I was in the nursing home rehab center after having my knees replaced and I still laugh when I remember one of these older ladies. I was coming down the hall one day after my rehab session when I saw her. I never even knew her name but she "knew" me. She was maybe 80 years old and wore her tightly curled once gray hair now slightly blue hair, with a flair. It was dyed that sort of pale blue hue that a lot of the hairdressers dye the hair of the elderly with. I complimented her on how pretty her hair looked and asked her if she had been to see Connie (an old friend of mine and hairdresser) who had a shop right in the rehab building. She said, "No, but my hair went to see Connie. My hair sits on my bed post at night." Her hair was a wig, of course. I nearly collapsed laughing. Lord, I miss meeting and talking to people like these I have mentioned.

One other story and then I'll stop. I knew this other older couple quite well and stopped regularly to see and talk with them. She had had a stroke and had given the cooking chore over to her husband. One day Mary got sick and Cecil tried to pick her up and go outside to their vehicle to take her to the doctor, but he fell on their steps and one of her legs was broken. From then on, the husband was the chief cook and bottle washer at that house. I stopped by one day and the husband was nearly in tears. I asked him what was the matter and he said he was cooking a roast or something like that for supper but didn't know what withits to cook.

I didn't have a clue what he was saying so I had to ask him what he meant. He said, "I know what meat I'm going to fix for supper but I don't know about the withits," he repeated once again. I found out he meant that he didn't know what side dishes would go with the meal he had planned. Now I know what someone means when they talk about withits. A perfect definition of withits to me.

If you really want to know how I feel about my time here in Brown County which spans 60 years now, you need to order two books I wrote in 2006 and which are still available on Amazon. One is titled "Appalachian Daughter," and the second in a series is titled "The Stuff of Legends." The first tells of my early life in the Pine Mountain area of eastern Kentucky, and the second book, tells of the 60 families who influenced me the most during these past 60+ years here in Van Buren Township, of Brown County.

I knew all 60 of those families and was loved by them back then and I still love their memory today. There are more books credited to me but these seem to be the most popular still after all these years.

My original early books are easy to read, they were written with nearly every family having an entire chapter to itself. You can read a chapter, lay it down and forget it for a while and come right back and pick up the thread of my stories. I wrote them in the style of a newspaper story. I just want you to promise to not dog ear the pages, just enjoy them to the fullest. Each and every one talked about in the second book The Stuff of Legends were truly legends to me and my little family.

There are many more books credited to me but these seem to be the most popular, along with a cookbook of Appalachian recipes and funny stories of my cooking disasters and lots of beautiful pictures called appropriately, "Grandma's Brown County Cookbook."

I have a really popular series of children's books that are just coming out now and are proving to be very loved by the children. My central figure is a big plump white goose named "Granny Goosefoot" who goes on fun adventures in every book. There is an interactive part and either a safety lesson or moral in each of the books. The latest ones I have written have several pages at the end of the story that the children can color either with their crayons or colored pencils. I have never seen this offered prior to my own thinking of it, but it makes sense and helps re- enforce the lessons taught in the reader portion of each of the books.

We are preparing the illustrations for this next book of Granny Going to the Empire State Building now. (It is now for sale on Amazon). In the first book Granny went on a cruise ship. My children's books were easy to write, I simply transposed what I had done and where I had been to Granny. I wrote these books during the Covid-19 outbreak in 2020 while my husband lay dying across the room in his hospital bed.

Anyone interested in my other books, they are all available on Amazon for a nominal price and quick shipment. Or, simply google my name on Amazon and all of my books will appear.

I try to keep some on hand here at my home for those who don't order from amazon early enough for the occasion they want to give a new book to. You are welcome to contact me.

So with this introduction to my past, I will turn my story over to you with the hope that you will enjoy reading more about me and about my stay in Brown County and in this book and what you can expect to see and learn if you make it a habit to visit us here.

Pack your bags and come see us.

THE LIAR'S BENCH

The Liar's Bench on the courthouse lawn has had a permanent place in our history since the early days of Brown County. It has been chronicled for history by noted photographer Frank Hohenberger, now deceased, who told the history of Brown County in his thousand plus pictures of life in Brown County.

An entire collection of his photos, taken many, many decades ago, are on file at the Indiana University library and many can be seen at the Brown County Art Gallery on East Main Street, Nashville, Indiana. He was the first photographer to document the lives of hundreds and hundreds of actual people at work, at home, doing crafts and arts or just by being themselves.

The Liar's Bench got its name mostly because in the early days of tourism in Brown County, it was usual to see a group of older men sitting on the bench on the courthouse lawn swapping stories with each other of what they had seen and heard or just fabricated themselves

about what was going on in Brown County. There would be uproarious laughter, knee slapping and backer (tobacco) spitting going on during these conversations.

Almost all of these men would be wearing bibbed overalls, any kind of old shirt or jacket depending upon the weather, a hat, (all men wore hats back then), and be wearing heavy brogan (work type) shoes.

It was a common scene but there was usually one or more of them who could tell more entertaining lies than the others, hence the name for this picture that has been duplicated hundreds of times. It was just one way these old men kept up on the gossip and news of the county.

The old men are all dead and gone to their reward now, but the bench can still be seen sitting on the courthouse lawn.

You too might be able to tell a lie if you sit on that bench!!

GIFTS TO OURSELF

It is estimated that there are 300 stores and restaurants in Nashville, each offering food, art, gifts, homemade crafts, and many other things of interest to Nashville's visitors. You can get your exercise by walking around town, in and out of the stores, or you can try a new method of exercising which we have gifted to ourselves.

For years and years Nashville and Brown County could not afford to merely gift itself with much of anything that costs money, but in recent years the coffers have opened up and we have begun gifting the residents of Brown County with things many of the old timers would never have thought about spending tax or grant money on.

One of those things is a walking trail that you can take at a leisurely or fast pace from Deer Run Park which begins just west of Nashville on West Main Street to the entrance of Deer Run Park on McClary Road, where the Salt Creek Trail begins. This little park is another of the gifts we have given the residents.

The Salt Creek Walking Trail goes east under the bridge across Salt Creek at the southern edge of Nashville, then along that creek all the way into the Brown County State Park, the largest state park in the state of Indiana. Then you can return the same way. I'm not sure of the mileage, but I would guess about six miles round trip.

The other gift I just mentioned (Deer Run Park) contains many amenities which have benefited all of us. It contains meeting places, playgrounds, ball parks, the new building we gifted to the veterans of Brown County where the veterans may gather or may want to leave some of their memorabilia on display there that they have saved from the military service during their terms of enlistments, and of course, the start of the Salt Creek Trail.

Yes, all these things cost money but with all the enterprises located nearby in Nashville and grants received from other sources, we are now able to think more strongly about our full-time residents.

Then, of course, I have mentioned the new Brown County Music Center on the other side of Salt Creek Park on Magnolia Lane.

We also have a beautiful, fairly new, county library. And on the hill right in front of that is our again, fairly new, courthouse annex. All supported by our tax dollars. And I can't forget the Brown County Playhouse which I mentioned earlier.

During a visit to my doctor in Bloomington several years ago he asked me if we had to pay county tax to which I replied, "Of course, doesn't everyone?" His reply to my response said it all. "As many visitors as you have in Brown County, they should be taxed enough so that no one has to pay taxes over there. Let the strangers to town pay your expenses."

It does not work that way or that easily, but it certainly helps fill the coffers when everyone pays their fair share of the expense of maintaining a small town and county like Brown County. I remember a few years back that the cost of toilet paper alone to supply the bathrooms in Nashville presented a big problem about the money with which to buy the stuff. The reporter who wrote the story dubbed it the "Tissue Issue" We are now able to do things for our residents that benefit them, not solely for the tourism trade.

There are about 300 bed and breakfast and/or tourist homes located here in Brown County and everyone staying the night here must pay a tax on that bed into a special fund which is used just to support this type of enterprise.

Probably the biggest expense to Brown County was the building housing the veterans office located in Deer Run Park. It is the first time in our history that something was dedicated entirely to helping veterans. It's the office of the first Veteran's Service Office to be had here in this county. It came about after the dedication of the Veteran's Memorial was erected on the Courthouse lawn in 1992 by this writer.

Over the years, I had collected the names of almost 2,000 servicemen and women who had lived in Brown County when they entered into the services, simply as a hobby of mine. No one had ever done anything about a memorial. I approached the county commissioners and asked to be granted permission to put the memorial on a corner of the Village Green, one block west of the courthouse. When the commissioners heard what I had done so far, they wanted it to be placed in the front entrance to the courthouse itself in the middle of town. So that is where I put the outside monument. Look inside the courthouse walls and you will see almost 2,000 names of those who served our country from this area. It took me years in my free time to collect these names, but I enjoyed doing this for our servicemen and women. My personal family has contributed a total of 91.5 years to military service, but they lived in different areas and are not included on the wall at the courthouse.

I agreed with them and formed a committee of veterans or their surviving wives to help me with this project. In less than six weeks I had gotten donations from enough county residents to pay for this monument, print a list of the names and which war they served in and if they were killed and what years they served.

Another veteran volunteer built several huge oak frames with glass fronts that were placed inside the entrance to the courthouse on the walls and all those names were pasted up on large sheets of paper at an industrial place in Indianapolis, then those big sheets were pasted inside the frames. An architect volunteered and designed the monument itself, and a stone quarry in Bloomington donated a portion of the cost of the stone, cut it and gave free delivery to put it in place.

I decided after the Persian Gulf wars to hold a formal dedication and wanted to invite an honor guard to partake of the festivities that day. Lo and behold, there was no formal honor guard in this county and since it was so close to Memorial Day none of those guard members

from surrounding counties could be on hand either. What to do next was the big question.

I asked some of the veterans and the funeral director if there was one and they told me no. I next approached the county sheriff and asked if they had one. He responded that they didn't have one but they should have because some of their deputies were old enough to die at any time and there would be one needed then. In the week prior to the dedication, those chosen for this work practiced and when the big day came, I got my twenty-one-gun salute from the deputies.

After that it was easy to finish this project with the result of the veteran's memorial building in Deer Run Park being erected and an office worker assigned to work there. Now we had it all. It made me very happy to realize that my habit of collecting veteran's names had finally paid off in a big way. Now if any veteran from any branch of service has a problem to be resolved, they can go there and get the help they need, all because of a habit of mine. Brown County was the last county in Indiana to appoint a Veteran's Service Officer.

We also have recently built an enormous Brown County Historical Building complex which contains several other nice things. A friend will tell you all about the Brown County History Center in the last chapter of this book.

I found the most amazing shop in my own opinion in Nashville located in antique Alley behind the Hob Nob restaurant among other places. That shop made the most wonderful chainsaw art I have ever encountered anywhere. I cannot describe it enough. Just take my word for it. You might need to be in a pickup truck for some of it but there were a few things this talented artist had carved, using only his chainsaw, but it would have to be described as art.

You can buy nearly anything from toys, food, gifts, leather items, tee shirts or balsamic vinegar or the candy and Ice cream. Surely there is something you desperately need and want. If so, you can find it in uniquely wonderful, Nashville, Brown County, Indiana.

This too, is who we are, unique, down-home people ready to help anyone who needs us. Bring your own chainsaw and get rich.

MORE ABOUT US

We also have a lot of dancers in our small community. Just west of Nashville and over the big hill there is a huge barn for dancing. Mike Robertson and his band play there on Saturday evenings most months except for the winter months or those months that were rampant with the Covid-19 disease. There will be a great performance by Mike and his other players to follow along with his yakkety sax which he plays wonderfully. I love to hear him play.

During the dance portion there might be nearly dozens of line dancers out on the floor and they will dance their little hearts out for about 45 minutes at a time then rest a few minutes and then go right back at it again. Monday evenings they give lessons to those wishing to learn how this dance is performed. It can be different in some respects to any song to which they are dancing. There is a minimal fee to enter and dance.

Another of our ventures is the Brown County Playhouse. It was given to Brown County I believe by the late Andy Rogers who was our resident mogul for many years. His children bought many of the businesses he owned at an auction after his death and are still operating them.

If you watch the local newspaper, you will see when and what is being offered by this venue. Sometimes, they might be showing a movie since we have no movie theater here in Brown County or if you are walking around and are on South Van Buren Street (state road 135) just stop by and inquire what is playing that night, if anything.

Often times, but not all the time, there will be live music at one or more of our town motels, such as the Brown County Inn or Seasons

You just have to look around, ask questions if they act or look like a local person and someone will tell you where you need to go to for information about this type of "wildlife." Through the week, it is difficult to find live music anywhere and many of the stores and shops close by 6 p.m.

This is just another example of who we are. Will you join us?

FREE THANKSGIVING DINNER

A way back in time in 1982 my mother died in March that year. For my entire life up until that event had seen all my immediate family and the nearby aunts, uncles and cousins and some other people from Eastern Kentucky usually spent each of the major holidays at our dinner table because mother was the best cook anyone had ever known, and we were too large a family of ten to go to someone else's home so they came to ours.

I had been married for a few years by then and had two growing sons, so I had never once thought about cooking all that food for just the four of us. But after mother died, it was a different story. There was no place to gather and eat that good food. What to do, what to do.

One weekend about a month and a half from the Thanksgiving holiday in 1982, I was visiting at the EMT headquarters in Nashville when another EMT came in with his wife and two children, both under six. They had the same problem as I had, no place to gather for Thanksgiving.

After much talking and discussing the problem, we made the decision to cook a free Thanksgiving

161

dinner for anyone who wanted to eat with us on the holiday itself. Now, we knew, most of the churches in the county would also serve a big pitch-in dinner a weekend or two before the actual holiday.

That would guarantee one big meal for our own planned diners, but since that was two or more weekends away prior to the actual holiday, there would still be the problem for many of our elderly people, especially, who would not have a gathering place on the actual date of Thanksgiving, so we decided to hold ours on that date ourselves.

That decision made we began to wonder if we had overstepped our abilities. Where would we get the money to buy the supplies? Neither one of us had that kind of dough. Where could we have it that would accommodate that many people. Oh, the problems and snags we managed to think about.

The chef of this one restaurant, Chef Ramon, had met with my partner and I and checked over what we thought we would be needing, and he asked us how many people we thought we would be feeding. We responded that we had no idea. He said to cook a lot of turkeys. The chef asked me personally how many turkeys I had ever baked, and I had to be truthful and told him, not a single one. People donated 23 turkeys to us so that was how many we stuck in the oven and baked.

We had no idea how many pies might be delivered and the night before our event when I finished baking the 150 pounds of cornbread for the dressing we would bake the next day, I went home to rest that night, nervous as a cat on a hot roof. There was not one slice of pie in that whole place. He advised us to bake 69 pies! That many was nearly incomprehensible.

The morning of Thanksgiving itself my husband drove me to the restaurant very early to get started. When I arrived, there were people sacked out in sleeping bags all over the floor, on all the sofas, chairs and other possible sleeping places. It seems there were several students at nearby Indiana University who had not gone home for Thanksgiving and had decided to come over to Brown County to help us. What a boon that was. Looking down a hallway away from the kitchen, I could see several long tables loaded down with little dessert plates with slices of pie on them covered with plastic wrap. The church women had come through for us.

On Saturday, the week before the holiday, this same restaurant had held an open house for the Brown County people and not one dish, pot or pan had been washed and put away. Dirty stuff was everywhere and then who would walk through our door but one man we all knew. He immediately told us he had experience operating a dishwashing machine and set to work, cleaning and scouring the entire kitchen clean and shiny.

Not a single one of us knew how to make gravy in quantity, I told him I could make gravy and he asked me in what quantity, and I said two cups at a time, but Chef Ramon told us we would need several gallons of it at least. A woman who worked with me at the newspaper along with her husband who had helped her run a restaurant in the past knew how to do this and set to work immediately making the gravy. Another problem solved.

And finally, another EMT showed up and asked to be the one to prepare all the mashed potatoes we needed. He read the recipe and made taters off and on all day and they all turned out very well.

As I finally felt like it might actually be going to happen, the Indianapolis TV station arrived and showcased our efforts. I was floored, but really glad they showed up before Santa Claus made his entrance and were ready to film Santa as all the children who were there swarmed over to Santa.

Our day was made. We had arrived. We had succeeded despite all the odds against us.

For the next 40 years that free Thanksgiving dinner on Thanksgiving day, has gone on without a hitch. I'm hoping we can make it to 41 years or more at least and it is possible we can do that. I'm so glad my friend and I decided to try this.

Most people who ate with us donated money after they had eaten even though they knew it was free to all. We donated all the money they donated and any left in the bank to the children's auction which is held in early December each year from the sale of items donated by the public. It guarantees every child in Brown County will have warm clothing and food and some toys for Christmas. The Giving just keeps on Going.

So can you cook? Come on Down.

OUR CHURCHES

There is a house of worship in every little burg in the county and several in Nashville itself.

Some sit way out along the highways and byways without a burg being around them, but they are utilized several times each week by those who know they are there.

Most of the ones that sit out by themselves or in very small villages are very plain but neatly built. Each has a sign outside denoting its denomination and anyone who wants to stop by and worship with them will be welcomed by the members.

I cannot think of a single protestant religion that is not represented in our area. None of the religions from other parts of the world are present in this county but can be attended not far away in Bartholomew County to our east. More are being erected in that county because of the diversity it has through its many industries which have so many ties to the foreign, to us, countries in the world. Bloomington, to our west about 15 miles, also has some of this type of service in part because of the vast number of foreign students living and studying at Indiana University.

One of the most impressive churches erected just outside Nashville is the Catholic church. It used to be north of town on State Road 135, but the congregation outgrew its space and this new one was built.

If you want to find it or attend at some time while here, it is located just west of Nashville's west Main Street. Go about a quarter mile out of town until you come to a hill. But before driving up the hill there is a little road to your left which is called McLary Road. Turn left and the church is not far from the intersection and will be on your right. There is a separate house for the Sister to occupy. All are welcome here.

Several new facilities have been erected in the past ten or twelve years in and around Nashville.

The one church that has been there seems like forever, is the little brick church on South Van Buren Street. It has white columns outside so you can't miss it. At certain times of the year they play Carillion music that you can hear all over town.

In addition to the regular churches here, there are about seven or eight church sponsored children's summer camps. One camp, Gnaw Bone Camp, played host to Vice President Dan Quail's child. They would arrive in a limousine entourage but didn't want to be noticed by the natives. I told everyone that if they had sent a dusty pickup truck with a gun across the back window, to the airport to pick up Mr. Quail's child, no notice would have been given. But a limousine entourage, with flags flying on the fenders, everyone knew of their arrival.

At any rate, if you want to attend a church of your choice while you are here, just ask anyone in any of the shops or stop by the Brown County Democrat newspaper office on east Main Street and they can help you find your way. The town is not large and we are all crowded together here. So just look around or ask someone who appears to live here.

Welcome to Brown County and may God Bless you.

Editor's Note: I hope you have enjoyed reading about Brown County and have learned how to be a Brown Countian yourself. I know this is sort of long but we are not through with this just yet.

PART THREE—
OUR HISTORY COMPLEX

I have asked Rhonda A. Dunn, an historical society archivist of some talent to give us all of what she knows of our Brown County Historical Society, one of the biggest and most active organizations in Brown County. Then we shall close this book

Welcome to becoming a Brown Countian. Now get your bags packed

Here's Rhonda!!

Rhonda was born in 1953 in Johnson County, Indiana, but with deep roots in Brown County. Her heritage goes back to the beginnings of the founding of Brown County in 1836, and she's always had a love for history.

Her father would take his family on weekend trips to Brown County to see his parents, aunts and uncles. Those visits were fond memories to see how her dad's family lived being poor farmers, and this was where she developed a deep love for the countryside and the people here.

Rhonda began volunteering at the Brown County Historical Society in 2006 and became deeply immersed in the local history of the county and its pioneers. Not long after, she was asked to take over the Archives. While the Archives is not a glamorous job, she came across so many interesting stories working in the Archives that she started writing stories to share with others of the stories she had found. "I thought everyone needed to know their own history," so she named the newly-born publication the "Brown County Journal."

She also belongs to the Genealogical society where she found out she was related to so many more people than she had ever thought. She also dedicates a good portion of her energies to the Cemetery Preservation Society which is now working on preserving the old abandoned and neglected cemeteries. Rhonda says she had never realized that Brown County's history was so interesting. "I am always thankful that my mother always prodded me to look into our family history, since it has become so very rewarding.

Now here is Rhonda's report on the doings of the Brown County History Center, probably one of the most active organizations in the entire county.

IT ALL STARTED WITH THE OLD LOG JAIL

It all started with the Old Log Jail, the wish to preserve our county history and treasures. The original structure was built in 1837 to house prisoners that were sent to jail to serve their time for offenses committed against the law and the citizens of Brown County.

The County `Commissioners appointed a committee to select two lots for a courthouse and a jail. In the old plat of Nashville, Lot No. 1 was selected for the Jail and Lot No. 2 for the Courthouse. Banner Brummett was ordered to let out contracts to build these two buildings to the lowest possible bidders at public auction. William Snider came in with the lowest bid for the Jail and David D. Weddle won the contract for the Courthouse. Both were to be built with hewed logs.

The building that was made for the log jail is why it is so appreciated today. The structure was laid out to be three walls thick with the outside wall of hewed oak logs 14 x 14 foot. A foot wide space between the inner and outer wall was filled with square timbers let down end ways.

It was a two-story building with seven feet between the lower and upper floors. One-foot-thick square timbers were laid down for the floor with a window on each side of the first floor criminal's room with "good and sufficient grates each way. The debtors' room was on the second floor as was a stuffed, two-headed calf. No one probably is alive who remembers why this particular calf was stored in the old log jail, but there it remains to this day. Criminals were to be let down into the first floor by a ladder and a hatchway in the upstairs Debtor's room. There was no outside entrance for criminals. A heavy iron door was the entrance to the building at the top of the outside stairway.

The original log jail was used up until about 1879 when a new one was needed. The present log jail was then built with similar specifications with the addition of an outside door into the lower room. The building was a little bigger this time being at 12 x 20 ft. The heavy iron doors were still needed and locked with a large iron key. It is rumored that some of the same materials and logs were re-used if they were still in good shape. It was used as a jail for prisoners up until about 1919 when it was retired.

The current log jail still stands and is a source of endless interest to historians and tourists. It was this most unusual structure that kept it in the eye of the county and its citizens. A long line of jailers and caretakers took on the job of keeping it in the public's eye. There are hundreds of photos of the old log jail with the jailors sitting in front guarding prisoners and giving tours to the public. To name a few of our more well-known representatives were Samuel Parks, Jason Skinner (a great uncle of Helen's husband, Mickey Ayers), and John Montz. It has been maintained constantly and refurbished quite recently.

In 2017 it was time again to give the old log jail some attention. It was decided by the Historical Society to look for someone who could do the job right and keep the building as historically accurate as possible. It just so turned out that a local man, Bird Snider, a descendant of the original builder, William Snider, was chosen to do the renovations. Bird having the same talents as his ancestors had the skills to do the job and he was so honored to be chosen knowing his family had a long history with the old log jail.

The next footnote in preserving our county history occurred when, what we now call affectionately, the Dog Trot building, was discovered. It is an old traditional English building plan, a log double-crib with an open-air walk through in the middle. The two cribs are joined on top with a second floor or roof line that spans the entire length.

Animals or farm equipment were probably housed in the individual cribs or "dogtrot" area. The upper level might have been used to store grain or hay, and it was dropped down through a chute to the animals. The farm family may have even used the upper level as a living space.

The story of how our Dogtrot building came to Nashville bears telling. In 1930 James Voland was rabbit hunting on property in Jackson County when he came across an old log barn that was abandoned. He bought the barn and along with his kin, Ed and Ora Voland, marked the logs and disassembled it to move to Brown County. The Community Club of Brown County bought the logs and went to work to get it reassembled on the two town lots where it now sits.

This occurred when the Great Depression hit the country and people were needing jobs. The government began the Works Progress Administration which put the poor and those in need of work back to work on jobs that helped the country. They were put to work reassembling the barn back together in 1936. The chimney and fireplaces were added at this time. It was used for many years as a meeting place for the Community Club and other organizations. After the club disbanded, the property's ownership went to the County Commissioners.

The management of the building was eventually handed over to the Historical Society, to keep it repaired and to start a museum. The Community Club had the idea that their town needed such a place as this for meetings and gatherings of its citizens. As it now stands, it is a testament to the forward thinking of our county citizens to gather, preserve, and put to good use things like this. That is the Brown County way. All of these events added to the idea that our history needed to be preserved.

In 1957 a group of about 30 Brown County citizens gathered at the Brown County Art Gallery to discuss organizing the Historical Society. This had been on many minds in Brown County. The first meetings were held in members' homes and then they began meeting at the Community Building. There were plans to have a museum complex on Helmsburg Road just west of Nashville, however distance from town and other problems led to the decision to instead buy the property at the old bowling alley north of Nashville.

In 1973, Dorothy Bailey was appointed to be the first archivist of the Historical Society. The search for historical data and records began. It was also during this time that the Curator Committee was formed. Items to furnish a museum were acquired, but with no place to store them at the time. Much of this was kept in member's homes until a proper place could be acquired to store and display them.

In 1972, the County Commissioners permitted the Historical Society to establish a museum in the former Community building. The Historical Society was to assume the responsibility for all maintenance that needed to be done on the buildings. The rooms of the old Community Building were put to use. A gift shop was set up in the lower west room for the

Pioneer Women to sell their crafts and books created about the history of Brown County.

The lower east room, called the Loom room, was set up to demonstrate the family arts such as quilting, spinning, and weaving with someone there on weekends to talk to the visitors and demonstrate their work. You can see Barbara Livesay on the spinning wheel every Sunday in this room; that is her passion.

 The large upstairs room was set up as the Museum with displays of antiques and pioneer home wares. An example of a pioneer bedroom with an antique baby cradle sits in one end of the room, a cobbler shop in one area, and miscellaneous other displays throughout.

The next acquisition was in 1975. An old log cabin was donated to the Historical Society by Violet David. It was a cabin that used to sit southeast of town down by Salt Creek. The logs of the cabin were numbered and disassembled and moved to the lot where the museum sits. A group of artisans from Brown County, the Plum Creek Restoration Company, rebuilt the log cabin assembling the logs back in their original state by the numbers marked in chalk on them. You can still see the numbers on the logs if you drive by. They used only the old-fashioned methods without any power tools to create the rest such as a roof and a fireplace. The cabin is now used as a display of an 1840s cabin furnished for a typical pioneer period. The Pioneer Women use it to give demonstrations of old-time family crafts.

It was not too long after the cabin was assembled that the Historical Society also received a donation of Dr. Alfred Ralphy's office. The two-room building was formerly located in the village of New Bellsville in Van Buren Township where he carried on his practice. With the help of a grant, it was loaded up and transported to the Museum complex and is now a functional display of an old-time doctor's office of the 1800s. Dr. Ralphy practiced as a country doctor in Brown County for nearly 50 years. It was a familiar site to see his horse and buggy coming down the road to make house calls to the sick and elderly. He was not one to take money from his patients if they could not pay but would take other things in trade if they had it. His office was built in 1898 by John Eddy. The building and all his instruments, books, and his journals were donated to the Historical Society by his daughter, Gladys Ralphy Whitaker, and Dr. Robert Siebel.

A blacksmith shop was built on the Museum complex property soon afterward and continues as a place to demonstrate the old art of blacksmithing in the summer months. The blacksmith shop is a replica of one dating from about 1850 with authentic tools of the trade being used. Jim Jesse, our resident blacksmith, will demonstrate how to heat and hammer metal into usable pioneer tools, utensils for the home, and farm tools.

Recent additions to the Historical Society are the fine new building that was built in 2014 and the replica of a one-room schoolhouse that sits on the lot directly north of the Museum Complex at 90 E. Gould Street.

An old smokehouse was donated in 2015 by Bruce and Pam Gould and was reconstructed 2 years ago. The Historical Society continues to grow its collection of pioneer artifacts, and new displays are set up periodically in the big new building, now called the History Center. It houses, besides many displays, a re-creation of the interior of a log cabin, a room to properly store artifacts of a delicate nature, an Historical Archives with accompanying research library, a Grand Hall for meetings, a gift shop, and a large room for our Pioneer Women to meet and teach the old-time fabric arts, such as spinning, quilting, weaving, knitting, tatting, and basketry.

The Pioneer Women's Club started as a wing of the Historical Society in the early days of our Society. They are committed to preserving the family arts. The Pioneer Women meet every Wednesday and is open to anyone who has a passion for the old crafts or would like to learn. Their annual Quilt Show has been going on for years and is a must-see event occurring every June.

The Historical Society is run by a Board of Directors with a President, Vice President, Secretary, and Treasurer with offices for all types of interests. The monthly dinner meeting is the first Monday of every month. Members, guests, and visitors are all welcome. The Mission Statement of the Brown County Historical Society is to "Collect, Preserve, and Present the History of Brown County, Indiana."

Rhonda Dunn, Archivist, Brown County Historical Society.

THIS IS OUR BROWN COUNTY

As far as I know, no one else has written such a book as this one giving the history of the whole of Brown County, so I did it myself with the help of Rhonda A. Dunn.

I cover most of the happenings in Brown County for more than 220 years up until the present time, making this book into three parts. The older part is from the 1800s. called simply, THEN. The stories since that time up to today, is simply called NOW. When we added the new history center information, we went to three parts to keep it simple to keep the history together for easier handling and reading.

Brown County has changed so much in 220 years, it is amazing. Most of what we are today is what we started from actually. Our early settlers were from the Carolinas, Virginias, Ohio and Kentucky. Many of those people or their offspring are still here today.

So, pull up a chair, grab a cup of coffee or tea and set a spell and read all about us.

ABOUT THE AUTHOR

I started writing stories when I was twelve-years-old in the seventh grade of school. I wrote an exciting story about saving my Grandmother from a coal mining slag heap that had begun slipping down the small ravine next to her home after being soaked from recent heavy rains. Heavy rains can be disastrous when falling on tall mountains, as all the water that falls, even a quarter inch, can cause havoc down below, and when loaded with rocks, mud and scrap coal its even more deadly.

I wrote about removing my grandmother from her home with enough blankets and quilts to shelter both of us and led her to the very top of the opposite mountainside. We stayed under shelter for hours and hours while the slag pile kept shifting downward and it was safe to leave the area in which we were sheltering.

Her home had missed the brunt of the slide which would have lethal to her and her neighbors, some of whom were not as lucky as the two of us. The battery-powered radio provided constant alerts about removing ourselves from the danger. No phones were available so the radio was our only communication.

I thought the story I wrote was a good one but my teacher had given me a C when I thought I would get an A at least. When I asked her why the low grade she told me she thought I had heard the story on the news and had copied it as part of my report. I explained that I was born in that area and stayed there until I was only six-years-old before moving to southern Indiana. Upon hearing of my background, the teacher changed my grade to an A.

This was the beginning of my writing career which extends to this day.

I credit this teacher with instilling in me the love of the printed word. For the first time in my life I had a pair of glasses that allowed me to read every book, magazine or newspaper I could lay my hands on since that pair of glasses allowed me to not be legally blind if I wore them. I loved to read books and give reports and when I had read every book in our tiny library I started in on reading several volumes of encyclopedias and the dictionary. At home I read the bible from beginning to end. Anything that was readable I read it. I still do that today.

I dearly love certain authors and have favorites I read again and again but I think I love writing those stories better than reading someone else's words. When I hear a child has begged to have more of my books to read it does my heart a lot of good. I hope the lessons embedded in the stories I write for them will make an impression on them.

And to hear other adults who say they love my history books and other types of things I write impresses me also. I appreciate every one of my books they like to read and tell others to buy.

Can you imagine being born legal blind and staying that way for the first ten years of your life while no one around you seemed to notice? I got my first pair of glasses when I was ten and for the first time in my life when I looked out the car window on the way home from the eye doctor I could see cattle grazing on the hillsides; there were small geodes in the little stream of water beside where we were driving; the green things I had seen all my life but could not distinguish were actually the leaves on the summer clad trees. My mother and my brother who were with me that day and, I admit, myself, all were crying.

It is hard to imagine today with all the things required to enter school you must have an eye exam, but it is a great thing to someone like myself whose eye doctor kept telling my mother to put me in Braille school. She refused and made sure we had enough money to furnish new glasses about every six months.

At any rate, times change, and most things for the better. I have been able to see now for decades of years.

So, I believe getting those glasses, having access to all the books in our school's tiny library and writing that story for the seventh grade teacher played a massive role in who I am today and what I can do.

With every book I write I tell people that the current one out is the last I'm going to do but then when I can't sleep nights for ideas running around and around in my head, I get out of bed the next morning and write until at least noon on a new book. I hope you like what I have done. The next several books to come out will be an influx of children's books and two Christmas themed books, many of which are being worked on by great artists.